Stormey
Knights

Breshea,
you are worthy of
everything you dream!!

Stormey Knights

Dominique Krystal Dawn

Write and Vibe Publishing
Cleveland

This is a work of fiction. All characters, organizations, and events portrayed in this novel are either products of the author's imagination or are used fictitiously. Any resemblance to actual persons, living or dead, is purely coincidental.

Published 2022

Printed in the United States of America
ISBN: 978-1-953430-13-7 (pbk)
ISBN: 978-1-953430-12-0 (ebook)

For information, address:
Write and Vibe Publishing
3675 Warrensville Center Road
P.O. Box 201372
Cleveland, OH 44120
cori@writeandvibe.com

*This book is dedicated to the wounded healer.
As you heal others, you heal yourself.*

CHAPTER 1

The Continuum

People wish for my looks. I'm only five-foot-five but I stand like nothing can knock me down. People are so consumed by my beauty, they're blinded. They look, but can't see me. Imagine, but can't fathom who I truly am. Some admire me. Others don't like me but can't figure out why. Some love me, while others think I need to be knocked down to size.

My hair is the blackest of black, flowing like water down my back, and softer than the finest silk. Boys say my perky breasts and curvy hips on my small waist are perfection, and men are mesmerized by my flawless mahogany skin and innocent big brown eyes. Women constantly ask if I'm mixed because my features are considered rare for a black girl.

The one thing that remains, they all think they know me. I find humor in how superficial people are. Their perceptions of me are misled by their delusions of what it is to be beautiful. But no one knows a damn thing about me, and they surely don't know my reality.

Would I be perceived differently if they knew I didn't know why my hair, skin, and eyes were this way? Would I earn their pity or condemnation if they learned I have no idea what I'm mixed with, or if I'm even mixed at all? Would I gain or lose their respect if I told them my mom is a prostitute and my dad is a faceless John?

Daily, I fight hard against the tides to stand strong, never allowing myself to slip into the patterns of those before me. The reality? I'm just one mistake away from being like the rest. I walk this way because of the hell I'm trying to escape. I'm afraid of slowing down because I can't afford to stop and feel life's pain. This is why I couldn't care less about any one opinion, good or bad. My sole focus is to escape the fears that haunt me. One day I hope to move so far away that my past can't find me. A place, that is much different than this one.

Growing up, I was told fables about self-respecting Blacks in America that carried themselves with dignity. Even after fighting long and hard to be seen as whole and complete human beings worthy of the elusive idea of equality, they continued to stand straight, look people in the eyes, and speak clearly.

Society was intimidated by their strength of mind. They attempted to dull their light by calling them inferior, but the attempts to convince them they were less than failed because these Blacks understood that their bloodline possessed the lineage of noble African Kings and Queens, therefore, they continued to wear their invisible crowns proudly.

Black men and women uplifted one another and treated each other like royalty. Getting married and creating respected families was a priority. Fathers lived in the household with their presence known. They worked, paid the bills, kept a roof over their family's head and made sure food was on the table. As men, each sacrificed their own needs to ensure the family never went without.

Mothers knew the depth of their innate feminine power and poured it into their families. They nurtured the spirits, cultivated the minds, and raised the children in the way they should go to ensure they never lost them to the streets. Boys were raised to be strong, respected, and respectful men, while girls were raised to be dignified, graceful, and discerning women. Every man was his brother's keeper because he knew that turning the other cheek to the injustices done to his brother would open the doors to the same injustices done unto himself.

Then, in the early eighties, the Trojan Horse arrived. There was a new oppressor in town; the white man was superseded by the white rock. A blizzard hit the Black communities leaving the streets overflowing with Crack Cocaine and just like that, souls were sold for a cloud of white smoke. With each inhale, someone lost a loved one. Fathers left their homes. Mothers abandoned their children. Siblings became strangers.

We chased down fool's gold to gain superficial success and sold dope to our own families. That spiritual genocide affected our children. Education became a burden. Children looking for guidance learned life lessons from rhyming words laid across a hot beat. Role models became far and few between. Kids began looking up to and mimicking reality stars on T.V.

We are engulfed in an era of auto-genocide, leaving us in a state of identity crisis devoid of any substantive culture. It seems like the further Blacks moved ahead in society, the further Blacks moved backwards inwardly. I know this was not too long ago, but where we are today makes the old days sound more like something from a movie.

I, too, am a component of this continuum I call, the Holocaust of Black America.

My mother fell to the Trojan Horse and has been hooked ever since. I don't know if there was ever a time of cleanliness or innocence for her because I've never seen her any other way. It's hard to imagine her with anything good within, excluding the times she was pregnant with me and my older sister, Skye.

People always ask the meaning for my name. Well, on the hot, summer night in 1998 that I was born, there was a roaring storm with violent winds. The thunder was so powerful it scared the crap out of my mom. From what I hear, she was in labor for all of twenty minutes and I was born before she even arrived at the hospital, but she was probably too high to know if she had been in labor longer.

There was hope that giving birth to me would be enough for my mom to turn her life around but it appears there will never be a storm big enough to cleanse her soul. She went further down the rabbit hole after my birth and I have yet to see her return.

My Aunt Jewel, my mother's older sister, entered my life with the essence of an angel. She gave a hopeless girl a reason to dream and she is the reason I'm alive today. I mean really alive, unlike how I used to be, walking around aimlessly, trying to survive.

I'm one of the fortunate ones, though. In the inner-city, where I'm from, no one comes back for us. No one cares to save us from our despondency. Somehow, they believe we earned it, that we deserve it, that we desire to exist in this state of agony. But what if it's deeper? What if there's more to our story?

I'm here to provide an offering. This is my chance to pay forward what my Aunt Jewel has done for me. She taught me how to see with more than my eyes. As she said, "What good are the eyes if the mind can't see?"

Journey through my world, with my sight as your guide. All I ask is that you put away your judgment and open your mind. It's time to understand that the generation I come from didn't just arrive full of chaos and hatred. We were made this way.

My name is Stormey Knights, and this is my story.

CHAPTER 2

Dimming Lights

As I'm riding the bus home from the mall, I realize that the scenery of the transitioning autumn leaves in this suburban neighborhood are dramatically more captivating than my own. Everything is so beautiful. The fancy over-sized homes and tall buildings are highlighted by the vibrant colors of the trees and the perfectly manicured landscapes, making it appear more like the backdrop of a movie than a place to live. There's no litter, broken, or boarded-up windows. No one is standing around aimlessly and the only noise I hear is traffic. I imagine what it'd be like to live in a well-to-do town like this where life is fear-free, neighbors are friendly, and the only beef is a little playful competition for the most beautiful yard. I yearn to experience life like this and I hope that one day soon I'll have enough money saved up to move into a quiet, safe, and peaceful community.

Just the peaceful thought of a life like this makes my eyes heavy and before long, I doze off. Confusion ensues as I find myself no longer sitting on the bus, but rather, in the midst of a violent storm. The confusion is interrupted by panic as I hear a horn blaring loudly. I look up and see a freight train barreling towards me as I am standing in the middle of the tracks. My hands grip a beautiful, purple, antique baby stroller. The train moves closer and the horn grows louder. Terrified, I push the baby stroller and leap out of the way. The jolted movement wakes me.

That dream was strange. The bus arrives at my destination and the neighborhood has drastically changed from captivating to revolting. The feeling of safety is replaced with unease as I hold the birthday gift I bought Skye as discreetly as possible. I hope I make it home safely.

While short-cutting through the park I observe a group of guys ending a game of basketball just as the streetlights turn on. The unwritten park rule? Don't get caught in the park after dark.

Foolishly, I used to think predators only preyed at night. However, last summer when my friend, Trina, was snatched in broad daylight, I learned that being out during the day was just as dangerous. Skye and I would see Trina every day while walking to and from school, until one day, we didn't.

At first, I didn't think much of it; I just thought she took the day off. But then I didn't see her the next day either. When I asked one of our mutual friends about her I found out Trina's own parents couldn't find her. She was missing, apparently snatched in broad daylight. I almost couldn't believe it.

Then, on another day, Skye and I took a different route home, which led us behind Trina's building. There, amongst the trash, was Trina's body. I stood there staring, cold chills running through my body. Skye quickly grabbed my hand and pulled me away. She knew it was best to pretend we hadn't seen her but I couldn't understand why no one else helped her or called the police. Someone had to have also seen her and they too, left her like she was nothing, like she never mattered.

Somebody knew what happened that day, but everyone pretended not to, preferring to mind their business. Had she screamed? If she did, had people ignored her?

Screaming, like gunfire, had become so common that it became more like background noise.

I never recovered after seeing Trina like that, but just like everyone else, I didn't say anything either. Soon after, the police found her body when they chased someone behind the building. But if they hadn't found her then, how long would she have remained there? Knowing that, on any given day, the same thing can happen to me, is terrifying. Every day I remain in the hood, I too, can become another unsolved mystery.

My aunt made me read, *The Miseducation of the Negro,* by Carter G. Woodson. In it, he wrote, "If you can control a man's thinking you do not have to worry about his action."

Most of the people in my neighborhood have accepted our perceived inferior status, and because we believe nothing will ever change, we don't waste our time trying to improve. That's why I have to move far away from here before my spirit becomes just as defeated and hopeless as my surroundings.

In front of me, a group of guys gamble under a hut-like pavilion, with a few thirsty females watching and waiting to prey on the winner. The game will end the same as they all do, with a fight. I quicken my pace as a guy wearing all black runs out of the hut towards me. I check my pocket to make sure I still have my blade.

"Hey, little momma, slow down. What's your hurry?" he says as he smiles at me.

I respond, "I can't. I'm already late."

He snaps angrily, "Well, let me walk with you. It's not safe for a pretty thing like you to be walking alone."

"Sorry, my dad will kill me if he sees us." I continue to speed walk. There are rules when walking around here. I call them survival tactics. Everyone can't handle bold rejection. The risk of being sassy and belittling someone can result in severe consequences, which is why it's best not to stop and talk. If caught in a conversation, be polite, but brief. I'd rather keep my life than lose it because of a fragile or overinflated ego.

When I arrive home, I take a moment to look at the yellow and white painted brick bungalow. As I walk up the five stairs leading to the sitting porch, I notice the paint peeling off the banisters, which is odd because Aunt Jewel religiously maintains the appearance of our home. She takes pride in appearances and doesn't usually let things around her fall apart or deteriorate. Before I walk inside, I glance at her bright blue rocking chair she loves to read in every morning.

Inside are Aunt Jewel's trinkets that she collected over the years from all of the places she traveled when younger. She has everything from seashells and gemstones to African masks. Walking through the living room is like going on a tour of her adventures. I hope to someday see half of what Aunt Jewel has.

The floors are all hardwood and freshly stained in cherry. Auntie had them replaced just before I moved in with her. Skye is already sitting at the small, round kitchen table talking and laughing with Aunt Jewel. After hanging my coat in the closet, I walk in to join them.

"Hi Auntie," I greet Aunt Jewel and hug her, then I turn to Skye. "Oooh, you got your lashes done. You look pretty."

Skye wears a Louis Vuitton embossed monogram leather mini skirt and matching bomber jacket. Her long honey blonde weave is styled with soft curls today.

"First of all, tell me when I'm not! But check out my brows. I just had them micro-shaded. They look natural right?" She pushes her hair over her shoulder.

I roll my eyes. "Girl, I don't even know why I bother but aren't you hot with that leather jacket on in this house?" As I hand her the gift, I can't believe I racked my brain for hours trying to get her the perfect gift just to feel like it's not good enough. "It's nothing fancy, I can't afford the things you like, but it's autumn and you need it because I never see you wear a scarf. So, this is the perfect season to start."

Skye laughs, "You've always been the thoughtful one. I love it though, so thanks."

"You have Troy to buy you everything you want so I have to be observant and get what you need," I say.

She quickly responds, "Well, apparently he hasn't bought me everything."

"You know what I'm saying. If you truly wanted a scarf all you'd have to do is tell him and you'd instantly have one from every designer."

Skye chuckles, "He is my man. He's supposed to take care of me and buy me everything I want."

"Well, I caught the bus to the mall to get this, so let that be a testament to who really loves you," I joke.

"You caught the bus?" Skye clutches her chest, faking a heart attack. "Oh, I can't believe it!"

I laugh, "I'm serious! You know how the fumes from the exhaust make me nauseous."

Skye says, "Girl, get your fake-bougie-self out of here. Acting brand new like you didn't grow up sleeping on the floor."

"I know you aren't talking. You used to sleep right next to me but since you got with Troy you've been dressing like you're from high society with all of your designer clothes, shoes, and oversized bags. So, who's really faking?" I snap back.

Aunt Jewel demands, "Okay, ladies, enough. You know I don't like hearing that kind of talk. I've told you before, where you come from, what you been through, the clothes you wear, none of that defines you. Your value is intrinsic and comes from within. Nothing outside of you will ever determine who you are or what you're worth. You decide who you become and how you experience life. Don't turn into human versions of junk food by letting money and trends define you. You'll know if you're living right by the weight of your heart. If you can keep it as light as a feather then you'll be happily at peace. Let's stop talking nonsense and celebrate."

Skye says, "Auntie, you know we're just joking."

Aunt Jewel responds, "Whether you're playing or not, words have power. What you think becomes what you say, what you say becomes what you do, and what you do becomes your reputation. Everyone can be a little foolish sometimes, it's how we grow, but don't be no stupid fool that never learns from their mistakes because you'll always be remembered that way."

Skye was about to speak again but I shoved her. I didn't want this to turn into another one of Aunt Jewel's infamous lectures. "Oh Skye, I almost forgot, I have a surprise for you." I quickly sprint to my room and back, proudly standing in front of Skye and Aunt Jewel. In my hands is a large painting I'd been working on for her.

"Oh my God, Stormey! It's me! You made a portrait of me! I love it!" Skye grabs the painting from my hand, holding it in the light to see it more closely.

"Stormey worked on it for days," Aunt Jewel adds.

"It looks exactly like me! Almost like a photo instead of a painting. Gosh, I wish I had your talent. You should think about selling your art. Like, open your own studio and get your work displayed in a gallery or something. You have too much talent to keep hidden away in your bedroom," Skye continues to gush.

"I will someday. I'm glad you like it," I humbly reply.

"Has anyone heard from Momma?" Skye unintentionally changes the mood in the room.

Aunt Jewel solemnly replies, "No, I haven't."

I don't want to kill the mood by talking about my mother, so I interrupt, "Auntie, show Skye the cake you made her."

She pulls out a homemade chocolate cake, Skye's favorite, shaped into the number twenty-two. I don't care for chocolate much, but I'll eat it today since it's a special occasion.

Skye looks at it. "Oh my God, Auntie it looks so good! I don't know why you be playing. You know you should've been had a bakery by now."

"You know I have skills in the kitchen but I'm too old to be chasing dreams. I'll leave that to you girls," she chuckles.

I glance at Skye, "You know Auntie doesn't believe in doing anything by half measures."

Auntie sets the cake onto the table, a grin on her face. "That's right. As you young folks say, go big or go home!"

We all laugh and Skye says, "Auntie, you're funny. No one says that anymore."

"Well, I do," Aunt Jewel laughs.

I prompt my auntie, "Come on, let's sing Happy Birthday."

We stand on each side of Skye and sing. As soon as we finish, Auntie tells Skye to make a wish. Skye closes her eyes for a few seconds, takes a deep breath, and blows out the candles.

"What did you wish for?" I ask.

Before Skye can reply, Aunt Jewel says, "Now Stormey, you know better. What did I tell you about telling others your hopes, wishes, and dreams?"

Skye and I sigh as we reply in sync, "To always keep them close to our heart until they are ready to be shared so that we don't give others the opportunity to negatively impact the outcome and make us doubt the vision God has given us."

She turns to Skye and says, "I hope you prayed for something big. You know what I say about playing God small."

"Auntie, you know I don't play small. I will have it all before I leave this earth."

"Well, the first step to achieving anything is to first believe you are worthy and capable, so you're halfway there. However, be careful of how you go about getting it. Sometimes the risk is too great, the consequences too severe, and the math just doesn't add up in the end."

This is where I would love to interject my two cents about Skye's relationship with Troy but before I can say something, Skye says, "I love you, Auntie. You are always the break of sunshine on a cloudy day."

It's obvious Aunt Jewel's message went right over her head but that doesn't mean she loves her any less. With Aunt Jewel being the rock of our family, Skye treasures her almost as much as I do and I couldn't imagine life without her. When Aunt Jewel came into my life, I no longer had to worry about what the night would bring.

Unlike my mother, when Aunt Jewel leaves, she returns. She is the woman I model myself after. Sheer perfection and no one can compare. When people see us together it makes me proud; they assume she's my mother because I'm the spitting image of her. She could have easily been a model or gotten by strictly on looks, but it's not only her external beauty, it's her entire essence. Men adore her. Women admire her, yet, she remains unaffected. She often says, "People are fascinated with outward appearances, but the prettiest face can conceal the ugliest heart. It is our job to be more than surface beauty by having strong minds, good character, and kind spirits."

A knock on the door brings me back to the current day so I get up to answer it and see Troy. True to himself, he's wearing his overpriced clothing that includes a leather jacket, designer scarf, Ray-Ban sunglasses, True Religion jeans, and Gucci boots. I try to hide my disgust, but it seeps out whenever he is near.

Skye is crazy about him. I'm happy she's happy but I don't like him. Other than him spending a ton of money on her, I have a hard time understanding what she sees in him. Troy is just one more poison-peddling drug dealer on the streets. I despise anyone so short-sighted by their own greed that they're willing to prey on another human being's weakness in pursuit of their own desires. There is no honor in the drug business. How does a person look in the mirror after helping others kill their souls? Or worse? When I see Troy, I see everything I hate in this world, especially knowing the effects that drugs have had on our mother. Drugs took her away and left us with nothing more than fantasies of who she was.

Aunt Jewel interrupts my glare when she yells out, "Stormey, who's at the door?"

"It's Troy." I look him up and down. He knows how I feel about him.

He laughs and walks past me, "What's up, Storm?"

"My name isn't Storm, it's Stormey," I say angrily.

He stops briefly. "I know what your name is. Storm is a nickname, but better. It's sounds cool, like the chick from X-Men. Stormey is childish. How do you expect anyone to take you seriously?"

"The irony of that statement coming from someone who's a walking joke. You have not earned the right to give me a nickname. So, it's Stormey to you."

"Wow that's how you feel? Okay Storm-ey," he chuckles as he makes his way to the kitchen.

"What's so funny?" I ask.

"You, youngin'." A sly smile pops up on his face.

I know he finds me amusing, partially because I'm younger, but also because he knows Skye is wrapped around his finger and he isn't going anywhere. Young or not, my intuition is sharp and I know when the devil enters the room.

Troy doesn't even bother acknowledging Aunt Jewel. "Skye, you ready?"

"Boy, you are just rude." The words rush right out of my mouth.

Before I can finish telling him about himself, Aunt Jewel politely interjects, "Hello, Troy. I'm glad you could join us. Would you like a piece of cake?"

"Nah, I'm good. I just came to get Skye." He looks at Skye and asks again, his impatience shining through. "You ready?"

Skye gets up from the table and puts on her coat.

"What's the rush?" I ask.

Skye continues to gather her belongings. "We have a reservation to get to."

Aunt Jewel stands. "I'll wrap your cake for you. Troy, would you like me to wrap you a piece as well?"

His tone, more clipped than necessary, is directed right at Skye. "No, we don't need any cake, can't afford to gain unnecessary weight. Can we Skye?"

Skye ignores him and hugs Aunt Jewel. "I'll be back tomorrow." She then hurries to catch Troy who's already walking out the door, leaving behind the painting I made for her. I hurry to catch her and when I get outside I see Troy fussing at her as they drive off in his white BMW coupe. I assume it's because she wasn't ready when he arrived and he had to come inside.

Disappointed that she left the painting behind, I stomp inside and stash it back in my room. When I join Aunt Jewel in the kitchen to help clean, she doesn't say anything so I break the silence. "I don't know what she sees in him. He's a rude low life. She left out of here without even taking her painting. When I get a boyfriend, I'll never let him run me like that. The only reason she latched onto him is because he has money. She's being the stupid fool you warned us about if you ask me."

Aunt Jewel replies, "I didn't."

I'm so wrapped up in my own thoughts that I'm not sure what she's talking about. "You didn't what?"

"I didn't ask you." She stops washing the dishes and turns to look at me. "Stormey, you think you have things all figured out, don't you? You shouldn't be so hard on your sister. She has her own battles to fight just as you do. We all do. When it comes to family, you need to learn to let them live their own lives and learn their own lessons. And as hard as it may be, you still have to be there for them when they need you."

I continue to clean the table, unsure of what has gotten into her. I don't know why she isn't seeing what I see so I keep trying to make my point. "You know something isn't right about him, Auntie. I don't feel he's right for her. He's overbearing, controlling, and everything she does revolves around him. She's changed since she's been with him and I can tell he doesn't have her best interest at heart because he expects her to jump on his command. I don't like who she's becoming and I know he's to blame."

Aunt Jewel doesn't utter one word. Once we're done cleaning, she sits at the table, looks at me, and points to the other chair. "Sit down."

I do so without speaking.

"Stormey, I know you love your sister. I understand how you feel about watching her go down a road you believe is not good for her. I watched your mother go down her own road and I'm still waiting for her to return. I spent so many days in pain and agony trying to get her to see what she was doing to herself. I would search for her in the middle of the night trying to bring her out of Satan's belly. I begged, pleaded, and cursed God for years as I cried myself to sleep at night."

I stared at her intently so she'd know I was listening.

"For years, I carried a burden that was not mine to carry. At the end of it all, each of us is here on this earth for our own unique purpose. I gave up on mine trying to help your mother not give up on hers. I tried to help her see in herself, what I could see so clearly. No matter what I did, or how hard I tried, I could not change her, and I could not save her. During that process, the only person who changed was me, and it wasn't for the better.

"One day I realized I had to loosen my grip and let her go. I have not given up on your mother, but I understand that sometimes people go through things that you just can't love them out of. I say all of this because I want you to know I understand your concern. I know what it's like to want to save your sister, but I need you to promise me something."

I look into her eyes. "Yes, Auntie?"

"No matter what Skye, your mother, myself, or anyone else you love does, promise me you will never stop living your own life. That you will never let the dimming of another's light dim your own. No matter what happens, continue on your path and never look back to bring others along who aren't going where you're going. Trust me when I tell you, their weight will become too much to carry and neither of you will make it. Instead, you will all remain stuck, together."

I take a deep breath. This is a lot to ask. My sister is my heart. Until recently, we were as thick as thieves and always by each other's side, but now, I don't know. Regardless, I give my word. It's apparent she's exhausted from the day, and possibly even life. She stands and gives me a hug.

"I have a migraine. I'm going to lay down and get some rest."

I softly say, "Okay. Feel better, Auntie. Goodnight."

From now on I'm going to keep my opinions about Skye and Troy to myself although my gut is telling me that she needs my help. Something isn't right and I don't want to wait patiently for Skye to figure that out.

I go back to my room and grab a blank canvas. Whenever I'm worried, stressed, or sad, the paint brush against the canvas brings me peace. Painting has always been therapeutic for me. As I paint, I think of ways to get through to Skye before she goes too far. But then, a thought creeps into my mind. What if Aunt Jewel is right? What if I get so caught up with trying to save Skye from herself that I abandon my own dreams of moving away and pursuing my art career, or worse, lose myself in the process?

Chapter 3

First Impressions

The blaring alarm clock flashing eight-fifteen A.M. prompts me to put down the paint brush just as I'm putting the finishing touches on my oil painting. I can't believe I stayed up all night. Today is my first day at the neighborhood diner and I'm going to be exhausted.

I scramble over to the closet to quickly find something to wear. Aunt Jewel would be disappointed if she knew I didn't have my clothes already laid out the night before. She always reminds me of how important first impressions are.

I grab my slacks, blouse, and a pair of flats, all in black because you can never go wrong with that. I iron my clothes and hurry to get in the shower because I have to be there in less than two hours.

It's exciting to think about the extra money I'll have to replenish my savings. I had to use a good portion of it to restock the art supplies my mother sold to support her habit. I'm still not over that. This time I will keep my money and my supplies far away from her so she can't smoke away my dreams as she's done with her own.

Clothes on, looking fly, I check the time. Being late on the first day is not an option. Thank God the diner is close. I grab the painting I created overnight as I head out my room. The aroma of food leads me to the kitchen. I sneak up on Aunt Jewel. "I made this for you, Auntie."

Her eyes light up. "Stormey, this is gorgeous. You really know how to brighten my day. I love it and I know exactly what I am going to do with it."

I hug her tightly. "I wish I could sit and eat breakfast with you but I need to make it to work on time."

"I'm already ahead of you. I made you a bag to go." She hands it to me and smiles.

"Aww, thank you. You didn't have to do that."

"I wasn't going to let you go to work on an empty stomach."

"You're the best!" I hug her again.

My job isn't far but I want to get there early so I power walk down the street, eating as I go. My breakfast sandwich of eggs, cheese, turkey sausage, and apple butter hits the spot and I devour it quickly.

The air chills my cheeks but thank God it isn't freezing out. The only problem is that the air isn't all that fresh. It smells horrible in certain parts as I walk past shabby and abandoned residences that are plagued with potently foul odors, which leads me to believe that if we look inside, we may find a missing person or two. I know that if the police ever decide to come by, they won't check anything and will instead, attribute the odor to water damage. I'd check for myself but I'm too afraid to see anything I can't unsee again. I hope I can save up enough money to get out of this God forsaken place soon.

Instead of focusing on the depressing scenery, I imagine my neighborhood with clean streets, well-kept homes with beautiful gardens, manicured tree lawns, and the aroma of freshly cut grass. Visualizing a better environment makes me feel empowered about my future.

The feeling is short lived as I catch a glimpse of a man driving a rusty blue pick-up with a familiar woman climbing into the passenger side. Is that her? Please don't be her. I stop in my tracks and stare harder to get a better look, suddenly feeling ill as my fear is confirmed. Amber Knights. Nearly a year has passed since I saw my mother.

The man places money into her hand and drives off, but not before my mother's eyes lock with mine. I hoped she wouldn't notice me, but I'm relieved she doesn't speak. I'm so ashamed to be her daughter.

Aunt Jewel says I'm supposed to honor, respect, forgive, and wish Amber the best because she's my mother. I know Auntie means well and she has never led me astray, but there are some things I have trouble understanding. How can I honor and respect her when she doesn't do the same for herself? Her choices have made it clear that she doesn't care about me, Skye, or anyone else, for that matter. I hate to be disobedient, but when it comes to her, I can't find an ounce of compassion. Over the years, the love I had for my mother has been lost and only a hollow shell of a heart remains.

I quicken my step and try to redirect my thoughts, not allowing her to ruin my day. I lower my head as I stride pass the three-level apartment building I used to live in with my mother and Skye. As usual, the front stoop of the apartment building is barricaded by the same group of guys. Although they stand around drinking and smoking all day, every day, they have an organized operation. They hang out, get high, and make money all at the same time. When someone walks up looking for drugs, one of the guys collects the money while another walks inside the building to the hidden stash and brings out the product. The customer leaves quickly and the cycle repeats.

The city streets have become the land of the heartless. Fast money is valued over everything. The paper chase has turned everyone into cutthroats and it's hard to tell friends from foes. The focus is on making money but none of it is used for cleaning or rebuilding the community. They don't even bother to fix their own homes either. They spend their cash faster than they make it on the latest sneakers and clothes with brand names they can't pronounce just to impress others and pretend they are doing better than the rest. Yet, at night their true feelings of deep unsatisfaction resurface as they sleep on floor mattresses. But I guess it's okay with them because in the morning, they start the process all over again.

"Hey baby girl, you good?" One of them, Jay, smiles from ear to ear. His complexion, dark chocolate with straight bright white teeth. Although I consistently reject his advances, he never ceases. I don't know why he doesn't put his energy into finding someone who returns his affections but he's a good friend. He doesn't bother anyone and no one bothers him.

"Yeah, I'm good, Jay."

"I haven't seen you in a while. What brings you 'round here?"

"I'm on my way to work. I got a job at the diner."

"Oh, you work for Mr. Haqq?" he asks.

"Yeah," I reply.

"How long you been working there?"

"It's actually my first day."

"Well, let me at least walk you there." Jay has always been protective of me. Even now, he's looking around us, making sure there's no trouble.

"I'm okay. I'm in a hurry and don't want to be late." Jay walks away. As I turn to walk away, I feel someone bump into me. I glance over and see the building's slumlord, Pete.

"Well, hey there little lady. Long time no see," Pete smirks.

My stomach instantly drops and my intestines knot into a pretzel. The sight of him is paralyzing. I thought I was over everything that happened but seeing him again brings it all back. Every memory from the night I left this building flood my mind as I glare into his eyes.

I was home alone. Skye had already moved out and my mother, per her usual, had been missing for a few days. I began to worry, thinking she had either finally met her match with a John who didn't want to pay for her services, or the drugs had finally taken their toll.

With no food, I left out, planning to steal something from the convenient. When I stepped out of my apartment I saw Jay's mother, Tina. She was next door begging her boyfriend, Tim, to let her inside his apartment. I could tell by the way she was moaning and pleading that it was time for her next fix.

Not too far away was Pete; he was checking me out. "You sure are growing up."

I pulled my door closed without acknowledging his statement and rolled my eyes into the back of my head.

"I was headed to your apartment. Is your mother in there?" Pete asked.

"What do you want with her?" I snapped.

"I came to collect the rent. Is she in there or not?" He asked impatiently.

"Don't you think you should clean this place up or maybe fix something around here before collecting more money from us?" I sneered. "What exactly are we paying you for? These living conditions are deplorable. There's filth everywhere, the stench of urine is all in the halls, trash is thrown all around, and I have to walk past dudes who don't even live here every day to get in and out of the front door. Seriously, what do you do other than collect money that you don't deserve?"

"I hear you sweetheart; it's a work in progress. Is your mother in there or not?" He pauses before asking, "Or should I just take my payment from you?"

"In progress? What have you actually started fixing? And don't think I'm not onto your manipulation tactics, putting pressure on us by turning off the furnace. I know you did that."

"I don't have time for this little girl. Where's your mother?" He pushes past to enter our apartment.

"Where are you going? She's not here!"

He turns back around after scanning the room. "You know, you are the spitting image of your mother. I bet you're just like her too."

"I'm nothing like her." I hold the door open, gesturing for him to leave.

"Nah, I bet you're just like her." Before I realize it, he grabs me and pulls me into him, leaning into kiss me.

I move my head, but not before screaming, "Stop! Get off me!" He slams the door and pushes my back against the wall, forcing his tongue in my mouth. His nails scratch me as he tugs at my pants until they're down. I knee him but can't overpower him. "Why are you doing this? STOP!" I fight as hard as I can, but am unable to break away. He slams me onto the floor and it's then that I notice this is all a wicked thrill for him.

"Please don't do this! Please!" I can't believe this is happening to me.

"You know you want this. You're your mother's daughter. It's time to collect."

Suddenly, the apartment door flies open and Jay bursts in. He pulls Pete off me and punches him repeatedly before dragging him into the hallway. I cry as I listen to the sound of Pete's body getting dragged down the stairs.

Jay saves me but I still feel violated. When Jay returns I try to say thank you but my words are stuck in my throat. Only the sounds of agony escape so he leaves, locking the door on the way out.

I crawl to my room and lay on the floor, wrapping myself in all the blankets I can find within arm's reach to keep warm. I cry for hours. Where is my mother? Am I so unlovable that she doesn't care what happens to me? I've barely eaten for days and am starving for not only food, but love and a peaceful place to safely rest my head. Safety seems so far removed, like an unattainable luxury.

I contemplate taking my life with a razor blade. I try to dig it into my wrist but ultimately, can't go through with the pain of cutting. I start thinking of other ways to kill myself that won't cause as much pain. As I mentally scan my options, I hear a loud knock on the door.

I assume it's Jay returning until I hear a familiar female voice. My Aunt Jewel.

"I've been calling for the last couple of days and no one's answered. Where is your mother?" She walks past me.

"She isn't here and must've taken the phone with her," I sigh.

"What? Why would she take the phone? Did she say when she'd be back?"

"No, she never does."

"Well how long has she been gone?" She badgers.

"I don't know. Maybe two-three days."

"Days? What! Did she say where she was going?" She asks.

"Never does," I stare straight ahead.

"Where's Skye?"

"Momma didn't tell you? Skye practically moved out and has been staying with her boyfriend, Troy."

"No, she didn't mention it. It's freezing in here. Is the heat on?"

"It's not working right now."

"When we last talked I thought everything was fine. Why didn't you tell me that you were living like this?"

"To be honest, I'm used to it and I didn't want to burden you."

"Okay, well, get unused to it. And for the record, you are never a burden to me. Pack your stuff. You're coming home with me."

For the first time, I feel hope and the relief that it brings. Hearing her words, I suddenly realize it wasn't death I was yearning for, but the pain of hopelessness to end.

No longer comfortable walking to the diner alone, I yell and signal for Jay.

"What's up?" He walks back over.

"I changed my mind. I want you to walk with me."

"Oh fa' sho," he says with a charming smile. "What's good, Pete?" Wry amusement is all over his body as he wraps his arm around my shoulder.

"How's it going, Jay?" Pete looks away nervously and walks off.

As we walk past the building I look at Jay. "I never thanked you."

"Thanked me for what?" Jay asks.

"You know, that night." Embarrassed, I lower my head and turn away from him.

"You know you're my baby and I'm not going to let anything happen to you."

"I appreciate you, Jay. I truly do."

"I told you I'm going to make you my wife, but you think I'm playing."

"Here you go with that. You really are something else."

"Hey, I haven't seen your mom home in a while, when was the last time you talked to her?" Jay changes the subject.

"I haven't," I reply. "Why are you asking about her?"

"What do you mean, why? Because she's your mother."

"Well, I don't talk to her. You would know more about her than me at this point."

"What do you mean you don't talk to her? Flawed or not, she's still your mom and she's the reason you're here."

"Don't remind me," I say sarcastically.

"Well, I was just wondering if she was cool."

"Now, you already know how she does her disappearing act. I'm sure she'll reappear in due time." For some reason I don't want to tell him I just saw her.

"Yeah, you're right."

Wanting to change the subject, I ask, "When are you going to get a real job and get out these streets?"

"The streets too good to me. I can't leave her, girl." He turns toward me with a flirtatious smile on his face. "Unless you give me a reason to."

"Oh, now you're making this about me again," I chuckle. "No, but seriously, doesn't it bother you knowing you're profiting off vulnerable people and helping them destroy their lives?"

"You're always on some Malcolm-X type of crusade. These people ruin their own lives. They want it, need it, are willing to pay anything, and do anything to get it. As long as they want it, I'm going to be here to supply them with it because if it isn't me, then it'll be someone else. Nobody's more deserving of this money than me. And as long as there is money out here to be made, I'm going to make it."

I nod my head even though I don't agree. This mentality is why we can never be together. "Well, we're here. Thanks again for escorting me. I appreciate how you look out for me." I give him a hug.

"Bet. Maybe you will let me take you out some time," he suggests.

"Maybe, Jay. Maybe."

"Love you, Stormey," Jay says playfully before turning to walk away.

I walk inside the diner without a minute to spare. Mr. Haqq is standing behind the counter holding a clipboard and appears to be checking the pie inventory. I hurry past, hoping he doesn't see me sneaking to the employee area in the back to put my belongings away. When I come out, he's still in the same location.

"Good morning, Mr. Haqq. How are you?"

"Good morning, young lady. I'm going to have you shadow Bree. She should be done with her break soon. You can sit out here and observe until then," Mr. Haqq advises.

Fifteen minutes later, Bree comes out wearing a white, short-sleeve, button-up blouse with a black tank top underneath, black form-fitting jeans, biker boots, and twenty-four inches of long blue flowing weave. Her makeup is trendy with long winged eyeliner and matte fuchsia lipstick.

"You must be Stormey. I'm Bree. Were you waiting a while?" She checks her watch.

"No, it wasn't long. I actually just got here. Mr. Haqq said I would be shadowing you."

She looks me over and asks, "How old are you?"

"Twenty-one."

She smiles. "Oh okay, I'm twenty-two."

"My sister's your age."

"Do you have any other siblings?"

"Nope, it's just me and Skye."

Surprise crosses her face. "Skye? Troy's Skye?"

"Yeah, you know her?"

She looks at me with a slight smirk and says, "It's not too many girls around here with the same name but, no, I don't know her. I just know of her."

My eyes narrow, "What do you know exactly?"

She assures me quickly, "Oh, it's nothing. You know how the streets talk. Everybody thinks they know everybody else's business." She changes the subject. "Let's get you trained. It's easy. You'll have it down in no time."

I'm still curious about what she knows, or thinks she knows about Skye, but I don't want to create tension. I grab a notebook and begin taking notes as she walks me through the register functions. After watching her ring out a few customers, she allows me to take the lead.

"Next," she says, "I'll show you how to take orders, but I can already tell you catch on fast so we're going to work well together." Looking at the clock she says, "I wonder what time they're coming."

"Who?" I ask.

Her face gleams. "Girl, these two guys come in here almost everyday and they're so freaking cute! One is about your complexion and the other one is milk chocolate with dreads. I've been waiting on the one with dreads to make a move on me, but so far, it's been a bust. I'm tired of waiting so I'm making my move when he comes in here today."

"You'd make a move on a guy?"

"Girl, time is waiting for no one. You have to go after what you want. Besides, he's so mysterious and I'm too curious not to find out what he's all about." She stares into space for a moment as if she's having some sort of fantasy. "Well, they called their order in to go so they should be here any minute. I'm going to run in the back really quick to check myself out before they arrive."

I continue working the register, unsure why she'd make so much fuss over a guy that hasn't expressed any interest in her. Besides, she's too pretty to be acting desperate.

Before Bree returns, a slender, elderly woman with curly silver hair and smooth brown skin walks over to the register to pay her bill. I make polite conversation while completing the transaction. "Hello, how are you?"

"Oh, I'm doing well. What about yourself?" She cheerfully responds while looking at the pies in the refrigerator next to the register.

"I'm okay. Do you want a pie to go?"

"You know what? I think I will." She points to the largest slice. "I'll take that piece of apple pie right there."

"Do you come here often?"

"I'm here all the time. You'll get used to seeing me."

The bells on the door jingle and I catch a glimpse of two guys walking in. I recognize them right away as the men that Bree was waiting on. They're more attractive than I thought. The guy with the medium brown complexion really does look smooth and glowy like caramel. He stands about six-feet-tall with a slim, athletic build, and low-cut wavy hair. The guy Bree's obsessing over is about six-foot-three with shoulder length dreads, broad shoulders, and defined muscles protruding through his shirt. They walk to the register and wait in line.

"Have a good day. I look forward to seeing you again." I hand the older woman her apple pie.

"Thanks. You, too, Darling," she replies.

"Good afternoon gentlemen, will you be dining with us today?"

The guy with the low-cut waves looks at me closely. "I've never seen you here before. Are you new?"

"Yeah, I started today."

"What's your name?" He smiles.

Mesmerized by how the light reflects off his perfectly straight, pearly-white teeth, I reply, "My name's Stormey. What's yours?"

"Stormey? Is that your real name?"

"Yes, it's my real name. And yours?"

"Ace," he answers.

"Ace? Is that your real name?" I mimic.

"Yeah, it is," he smiles.

Bree comes walking toward the register as if her primal senses have been alerted. I notice she's only looking at the guy with dreads. "Have you guys been taken care of?"

He responds, "We're good."

"You come in here all the time, but I don't know your name," she says.

"Black," he replies dryly.

Bree continues, "How mysterious."

Ace, who hasn't taken his eyes off me, says, "We ordered our food to go. It's under the name King."

"I'll check to see if it's ready," says Bree.

Ace looks at me, thinking a bit before asking. "What time do you get off?"

"Now why do you need to know that?"

"So I can pick you up."

"I'm not going anywhere with you. I don't even know you," I sassily reply.

"Well, when are you free so I can take you out?" he persists.

"I'm not dating right now."

"Don't worry, I'll change that," he says confidently.

"Are you sure about that?"

"You'll see."

Bree places their order on the counter. "Your total is twenty-four ninety-seven."

Black turns around at the sound of the bells on the door. An older guy walks in while talking on the phone. He gives him a head nod. Black nudges Ace. "Yo, King's ready." He pulls out a large wad of cash and puts two twenty-dollar bills on the counter, uttering, "Keep the change."

"I'll be back for you." Ace winks at me and grabs their food. They hustle to the door, following behind King, who is still on the phone. While exiting, Ace stops to hold the door for an elderly couple.

After they leave, Bree screams like a little schoolgirl. She gathers her composure and says, "Oh, my God, girl! I cannot believe you didn't give him your number! What were you thinking?"

I shrug, "He didn't actually ask for my number and besides, I don't want to date right now."

She says, "Girl, he has money! You better jump on him before someone else does."

"I don't care about that. What does money have to with anything, anyway?"

She continues, "I mean, why though? Did you just get out of a relationship? Are you still hung up on your ex or something?"

"No, I just don't have time for guys right now."

"Why not? What you got going on?"

"Nothing. I know they are only looking for a good time and I take myself too seriously to be playing games."

Her mouth open, she finally says, "Girl, everyone is looking for a good time or else what would be the point? Besides everybody wants sex, not just guys."

I shake my head. "I'm not like everyone else and I'm not interested. Okay?"

She chuckles, "Oh my God! I didn't know your kind still existed."

"My kind? What do you mean?"

"You know, the wannabe good girl thinking you're special type. Well, you better use that thing before it grows cobwebs! You're getting too old for needing to be taught how to perform," she continues to mock.

"Performing? I'm not performing for anybody. Besides, these guys will say anything to get what they want. So, excuse me for not jumping for joy because he thinks I'm cute."

"Girl, whoever messed you up did a real number on you," Bree says.

Bree's statement causes me to become aware of the dormant anger behind my words. She's only telling me her opinion, but I'm deeply offended. I'm not upset with her, I'm angry because nearly every John I've seen my mother with was wearing a wedding ring. They would have sex with her and then return home to their unsuspecting families. I'm angry because I can't imagine any man ever touching me after what Pete did to me.

Being in a position where I was void of choice made me value the power of *no*. Before I was assaulted, I might have listened to Bree and probably agreed with her. I hadn't thought about my virginity or how I'd lose it or who I'd lose it to. Now, I don't take losing it lightly. I don't know when or if I'll ever be ready to trust anyone enough to let it go.

Bree may be older than me, but it's obvious she hasn't seen or experienced as much because she's quite immature. "Look, I hope someday I meet a guy who'll prove me wrong. But so far, I haven't," I say to her.

"You'll never find him with that attitude. They'll have to fight through the fortress you've built around yourself," she states.

"Yeah, maybe."

"Well, whatever, Black is mine," she says.

I roll my eyes. Black barely even looked at her. "I want to be with the one for me, not the one that is only with me for the moment. I want to remain exclusive." I respond, hoping I sound less bitter.

"Exclusive! Girl how do you expect someone to want to be exclusive with you and you don't even know how to throw that thang back!" Bree laughs while popping her hips. If you trying to get locked in then you better already know how to please your man. And how do you expect to do that if you're not practicing?"

I look at Bree sideways, full of judgment. "Practicing? Is that what you call it? I'm not auditioning for a temporary role with some guy whose only concern is how it feels to be inside of me. I'll leave those things to puppets."

Bree freezes. "Puppets? What's that supposed to mean?"

I laugh, "Look, it's too soon to be having a deep dialogue, we just met. I'm not saying I'm better than anyone else, but a wise woman once said that you teach people how to treat you by what you accept, tolerate, and accommodate. So, I don't intend on settling for only what someone wants to give me or thinks I should have. I'll only accept what I want. However, puppets are people that get their life advice from memes on social media and let the world tell them how they should expect to be treated even if it goes against what their soul knows. I've learned that acting common gets you treated as if you're nothing special. And who wants to be treated like they are not worth it?"

My phone rings and I'm relieved. "Hey this is my ride..."

Bree cuts me off. "You can go now. Five more minutes won't make much difference. Mike is here to help me close anyway."

"Thanks. I appreciate you being cool. I'll see you tomorrow." I grab my belongings, walk outside, and see that Skye is driving Troy's car. I hop into the passenger side. "When did Troy start letting you drive the coupe?"

"I always drive it but today I have to hurry and take it back home to him after I drop you off."

"Does he know you have it?" I ask curiously.

Skye laughs, "Of course he knows I have it."

"Oh, well you know how you like to live on the edge."

"Girl, Troy's all talk. He wouldn't do a thing except fuss at me and I'd ignore him as I always do."

"I always hear it starts verbal before it turns physical. I wouldn't do anything to push him if I were you," I advise. We pull in front of the house and see Aunt Jewel on the porch rocking in her chair.

"Hurry and get out. I gotta go." Skye then yells from the car, "Hi, Auntie! I have to run, but I'll be back later."

Aunt Jewel waves back. "Okay."

I get out of the car and walk toward the house. Skye drives away as she blows the horn. I can't help but feel like she's up to something, but I shake it off and go inside. I've had a long day at work and the only thing I want to do is take a hot shower.

CHAPTER 4

Watchful Eyes

Aunt Jewel's warning about being so focused on Skye that I lose sight of myself won't get out of my head. Her reminder to never let the dimming of another's light to dim mine are steadily ringing in my ears, worrying me almost as bad as last night's nightmare. I dreamt Skye was in trouble and needed help but I didn't know where, or how to find her.

I've been calling her but she's not answering and I'm starting to get nervous. It's not like her to ignore my calls. Regardless of the time, she always answers. I'm going to drive myself mad from worrying about her.

"Stormey!" Jay walks into the diner with his arms in the air as he greets me with a smile.

"What's up, Jay?"

"Nothing. Just checking on my favorite girl." He takes a seat at the counter where I'm standing.

"Well, you can't just come and chill. You gotta order something," I warn him.

"Don't be like that, I'm ordering. Pass me a menu."

"Just making sure you don't get too comfortable because this *is* my job." I hand him a menu. "Have you seen Skye around?"

"Nah, I haven't seen her in a minute. She doesn't come 'round the hood much since she's been kicking it with ol' boy." He looks over the menu.

"What do you know about Troy?" I inquire.

"Nothing for real. He's from the other side of town. You know we don't mess with them over there," he answers.

"No one seems to know much about him."

"That's a good thing for him," Jay comments.

"But that's what has me worried. I don't trust him."

"What's there to worry about?"

"It's just a feeling I got and Skye isn't answering my calls."

"Your sister isn't like you; she can handle herself. You sure you're not just upset because she finally has a life that doesn't revolve around you?"

Insulted, I ask, "What's that supposed to mean?"

"Nothing," he says nonchalantly. He points at the menu, "I'm going to order this."

"It's almost six o'clock in the evening and you're ordering breakfast, Jay?"

"It says *all-day breakfast*. Y'all wouldn't sell it all day if I was the only one ordering it after hours," he responds.

The bells on the diner door jingle. I look up to see Ace walk in with Black and King. King asks them, "Do y'all know them young dudes standing in the parking lot?"

Ace looks at the guys through the window and asks, "Nah, what about them? They just look like two dudes hanging out."

Black sits in a booth, King and Ace join him. He responds, "Why? What's up with them?"

Although King is fit and doesn't look a day over thirty, I notice a few grey hairs glistening under the diner lights, proving he's older than he looks. He points his finger at them. "I watched both of you walk past them twice but neither one of you looked up once. Ace, as my son, and Black as my number two, y'all both have to do better and pay attention to your surroundings. You have to watch your back and front at the same time. These dudes out here got nothing to lose, but everything to gain if you get caught slipping. You both are too important not to be on guard at all times. If y'all can't see the watchful eyes around you, then you've already lost."

"You know them?" I ask Jay.

"You don't know who that is?" Jay asks with a confused look on his face.

"No, I just seen them for the first time yesterday when they came to get something to eat," I respond.

"Do you remember the dude that came to the hood giving out turkeys and toys to all of the kids last year?" Jay asks softly.

"I remember hearing about it," I answer.

Jay talks low enough for only me to hear him. "Well, that's him, King. He's the H.N.I.C. and he runs everything around here. If anyone is doing anything on this side of town, it's because he's allowing them to. Nothing happens without his consent. He's the guy that everyone on the block aspires to be. In fact, he owns the block, literally. Mr. Haqq and all the other business owners in this lot rent their space from him."

"I should've known they're drug dealers," I scoff and roll my eyes.

"Out of everything I just said, that's what you heard?" Jay shakes his head as he continues filling me in. "I went to school with the younger of the two dudes. The one with dreads name is Tyshawn, everyone calls him Black, but it's more so because of his cutthroat mentality than his complexion. He's King's enforcer and doesn't have a sympathetic bone in his body. When Black comes around everyone straightens up quick. The other guy is King's son, Ace. King keeps him clean. He works at the wash a few doors down from here. I'm gonna go speak." Jay gets up from his seat at the counter and walks over to join their conversation. I grab a rag and wipe down the tables so I can eavesdrop.

"What's up, O.G.?" Jay greets King.

"What's going on, youngin'?" King responds.

Jay shakes Black's hand and gives Ace a head nod. He continues, "I heard about Rocco. My condolences."

"Thank you," King solemnly states.

"I can't believe he was caught slipping like that. No disrespect but since your second in command is gone, who's going to take his spot?" Jay asks.

"You're looking at him," Black confidently states.

"The same thing is going to happen to you if you keep believing your own hype and walking past new faces without looking. Being too comfortable and too trusting is a death sentence," King warns.

Black responds, "For real? You going to wish bad on me like that?"

King says, "I'm not wishing bad on you. I'm only telling you what's inevitable. Every move you make has consequences. The only way to prevent getting caught is to pay attention to the watchful eyes around to see how they're really looking at you."

Black huffs, "These cats know how I get down. They know better than to come for me. My name carry heat in the streets."

King looks at him. "You're making my point. That's why you have to look deeper, because if you don't, you won't know who is who, or who to trust. If you pay attention, you can see the smiles on their faces and the envy in their eyes at the same time. Ain't no more loyalty or honor out here, just a bunch of cowards waiting to take what you got. That's the cost of living well amongst miserable people."

"Like I said, they know better than to try me," Black shuffles in his seat.

King asks, "How old are each of you?"

Jay says, "I'm twenty-two."

Black answers, "Twenty-two."

"Twenty-one, but you know how old I am," Ace chuckles,

"You all are in your early twenties so naturally, you take a lot for granted that you shouldn't. It's not saying anything bad about you because we all take things and people for granted when we're young. But when you take on this lifestyle, and Ace, because you're my son, you have to stay alert and aware of your surroundings no matter where you are, no matter how comfortable you have become in your environment. Always watch the eyes around you because the eyes of the one that loves you becomes the eyes of the one that hates you. The eyes always change even though the face remains the same. Don't make the same mistake Rocco made. Don't believe that you can trust a face just because it's been around for a long time. Watch the eyes or else these cowards will make a fool out of you, or even worse, do to you what they just did to him."

"What do my eyes say to you?" Black stares at King intently.

King replies, "They say that you think you're smarter than you are. But you know what they say about having a hard head."

"My circle is tight. I don't have them kind of problems, everybody loves me," Black says.

"Don't get caught up in the daydream or be deceived by the love you find in the streets because just like candy, it's artificially sweet. Ain't no friends in this business. That same so-called circle will get you twenty to life. All you have is each other. Don't fall victim by bringing outsiders in."

"Nah, never that. I know better," Black responds.

"I hold my cards to my chest tight," King says. "I don't tell anyone anything that isn't absolutely necessary or pertinent to their role in the business. No one has knowledge of anyone else's job. I don't do business without anyone I haven't checked thoroughly. The right hand never knows what the left hand is doing and that's why I'm where I am today. I've never been to jail and never will because I keep everyone out of my business. I'm not friendly, chatty, nor greedy," says King.

"And that's why you are the O.G.," Jay raises his right hand to salute.

"Yup," interjects Black.

King advises, "If it was up to anyone else I wouldn't have made it this far. There's no secret recipe. Do whatever it takes to survive. As long as you're surviving, the rest don't matter. Remember, the victor is the one that tells the story. Make sure you're around to tell the version you want everyone to know."

Black replies, "Tell me something I don't know. Everyone talks like they are built like the man of steel until they are facing time behind that iron. Then they trade in their cape for a purse and start squealing like little girls."

"Preach!" Ace replies.

"Don't listen to him," King says. "That's why I pay that expensive tuition for you to attend Prestige University and get your Bachelor of Science in Business so you don't have to worry about the same things we do," King says. "How are your classes coming along, anyway?"

"This is my last year, so I'm finishing strong," Ace responds.

"That's what I like to hear. Make your old man proud," King says, almost bursting with pride.

"I see you college boy," Jay nods his head with approval.

"Yo! Prince Charming, look! There goes Cinderella," Black teases Ace.

I blush. He's talking about me but I don't want them to know that I know so I turn away and pretend not to hear.

"Who, Stormey?" Jay asks while glancing towards me with a jealous look on his face.

"Dude, you got jokes," Ace responds and gives an embarrassed chuckle.

King, who's obviously agitated, says to Jay, "Alright, that looks like your food. I won't hold you."

"Alright. I need to come through and check on that one thing this week," Jay speaks in their coded language.

"Bet," King responds.

Jay returns to his seat at the counter where his food is waiting.

"Your boy's game needs major work. You should've seen him trying to get that server's number. His failure was epic," Black says, taunting Ace.

Out of things to clean near them, I walk back over to the counter where I can still hear them talking.

King chuckles, "What happened?" Black just shakes his head.

"We had to leave, but I'll get her. Watch me," Ace says.

"I like that determination in you son," King says.

"Look at her, isn't she gorgeous?" Ace asks King while looking fondly at me.

"Man, calm down. She's alright. You act like you're falling in love already," Black states.

"Stop hating, Dude, and find ol' girl that was drooling all over you," Ace responds.

"Nah, I'm good and what I got to hate for? I would've got her the first time," Black says.

"Here he goes," Ace says.

Black continues, "Two words, high school. You couldn't see me then and you can't see me now. I bag the chicks you fantasize about. Have you even been with a girl yet?"

"For real, now you want to play me? You should know best because you kept running behind me like it was an award being given out for getting with my sloppy seconds," Ace defensively replies.

Black asks, "You still mad, huh?"

Ace answers, "We're close but I don't ever wanna be that close. You move so foul sometimes I don't even know why I deal with you."

Black laughs, "If you're done with them then what difference does it make?"

King replies, "None, if you were up front about it."

Black responds, "You need to tell your son to stop getting his feelings caught up in these females."

King replies, "A woman can be the source of a man's pride or his downfall. You have to choose the one you crown carefully. If you chose wrong, she can cause you to lose everything."

"Stormey! Yo, Stormey!" Bree shouts.

"Yeah?" I look toward her, puzzled as to why she's so excited.

"Why didn't you tell me they were here?" She whispers, eyeballing Ace and Black at the table.

"I didn't know it was that serious," I respond nonchalantly.

"I don't know why you act like that," she scoffs and rolls her eyes.

"She's mine anyway," Jay interjects.

"I'm not your nothing," I slap his arm laughing.

"I told you, we getting married. I ain't playing," Jay smiles flirtatiously.

"Stormey, who's this?" asks Bree.

"This is my friend, Jay. We've known each other since forever."

"Well, you know people that grow up together make the best lovers. You've grown roots and are less likely to hurt each other," Bree carries on.

I shake my head with annoyance. "Girl, would you sit down somewhere and stop turning everything into a romance novel?"

"Yeah, okay, but when you're old and lonely with your cats, you're going to wish you would've listened to me."

"I seriously doubt that."

Jay looks at his phone. "I gotta run, when are you working again?"

"I work tomorrow, three to close."

"Alright, I'll try to come by and see you."

"Nice meeting you," Bree smiles.

I clean off the counter where Jay was eating but Bree nudges me in the arm. "Here he comes, girl."

I look up to see Ace approaching so I try to hurry up and walk away with the dishes.

"I'll take those," Bree smirks. Stuck, I turn around and quickly wipe the counter again.

"How's your day so far?" Ace asks.

"It's been long. I'm tired. Can't wait to get out of here."

"What time you get off?"

"I'm off now but I'm waiting on my sister. She should've been here by now." I look at my watch.

"Have you tried calling her?"

"Yeah, she's not answering." I spot Black and King walking towards the door. "You know they're leaving you, right?"

"I'm not going with them today. I gotta work."

"What do you do?"

"I manage the car wash a few doors down."

"How long have you been doing that?"

"Since high school. It's not the only one I manage though. We have four of them," he explains.

"Who's we?"

"Me and my uncle Tone," he replies.

"Oh, so it's like a family business?"

"Yeah, you can say that."

"Is he your uncle on your dad's or your mom's side?"

"Neither actually. Tone and my dad been friends since elementary school. I call him uncle because he's been around my whole life."

"Oh, so you work for him?"

"It's complicated."

"What's complicated? Either you work for him or you don't."

"Well, I'm working on becoming a partner."

Bree comes from the back and interrupts, "You still here? I thought you would be gone by now."

"Me too," I say sarcastically.

"I can give you a ride. I promise I won't bite," Ace jokes.

"No thanks. I'll figure something out," I reply.

"Well, here, take my number just in case you change your mind." He writes it down on a napkin and passes it to me.

"Thanks." I put the napkin in my pocket as Ace leaves.

Bree leans on the counter and asks, "So, what are you going to do?"

"I'm gonna get an Uber."

"Why would you get an Uber when he was offering you a ride? I swear you are difficult for no reason," she snarks.

"Because I don't jump in the car with people I don't know."

"But you're riding in an Uber," she says sarcastically.

"It's not the same thing."

"Tell me how it's not."

"They should be pulling up soon. I'm going to wait outside."

When I get outside, Ace is talking to a man standing outside of an eggplant-colored Mercedes on rims. "What's good, Rich? I appreciate your business. You keep this baby gleaming." Ace gives him dap.

"What's good, Lil' King? I see you serious about this car washing business," says Rich.

"Yeah, trying to keep the 'hood looking good," Ace replies.

"What I don't understand is how your father is King and the prince is out here waxing cars," Rich says.

"I'm good where I'm at," Ace says.

"You ever wonder why he choose Black as his right hand instead of his own son? I'd feel slighted if I were you."

"Well, it's a good thing you aren't me," Ace snaps.

Rich is relentless. "Black says you're weak, but I beg to differ. You could come hang with me Lil' King. I'll take you in and show you a few things. When I get done, you surely won't want to go back to that carwash and sweat for less anymore."

"I'm good," Ace says sternly. "And since when did you start talking to Black?"

"There I go saying too much." Rich walks back to his car and before he gets inside, he turns back and reiterates, "You know where to find me if you change your mind." He drives off.

Ace sees me and asks, "You alright? Ever get in touch with your sister?"

"I'm okay. My ride is on the way," I answer.

"Well, I'll wait with you, make sure you're safe," he says.

"Who was that?" I ask.

"Nobody," he says.

"Well, for him to be nobody it sure seems like he upset you," I pry.

"Just thinking about something my father said about keeping a watchful eye."

"There's my ride. Thank you for waiting with me."

"Of course. I would be less of a gentleman if I didn't." Ace opens the rear passenger door for me.

"I may have misjudged you Ace. I'm going to text you my number." I get into the car.

"I'll be waiting." A big smile covers his face and he closes the car door for me. I assumed he was like his father but as it turns out, he actually may be different.

CHAPTER 5

Open Wounds

Aunt Jewel is already up; I smell the bacon cooking. My mouth is watering just thinking about eating grits with cheese, bacon, scrambled eggs, and my favorite, sweet potato pancakes.

For a moment though, I continue lying in bed, captivated by the warmth from the sun's rays brushing gently like velvet across my face. Overcome by a rare, faint sense of comfort, for a flash, I feel whole, complete, and happy. Each morning I long to savor this feeling because for a split second, I can't feel the tightness in my chest or the worry in the pit of my stomach. I forget how I'm fatherless with a drug-addicted mother that cares more about her next high than her own family. I forget that my sister, who once was my best friend, has begun evolving into a stranger more and more with each passing day. I forget that my existence feels like constant suffering and secretly I hope each breath will be my last. I forget my prayers have been left unanswered as I have been ignored, neglected, and cast aside by God. I forget it all in this brief moment. Just for a flicker, I forget, that I've been forgotten. I sigh deeply as I roll out of bed to make my way to the kitchen before the food gets cold.

"Good morning," I greet Aunt Jewel as she stands, cooking in her purple and turquoise nightgown.

"Good morning," she replies with a warm smile.

"Do you need any help with breakfast?"

Joyfully she says, "No, but thanks. I'm almost done."

Just as I start to sit down, someone knocks on the door. I sigh, "I'll get it." I look out the peephole and see it's Skye. "I should've known it was you. Did your Spidey-sense tell you Auntie was cooking breakfast?"

Grinning like the Cheshire Cat, Skye says, "I didn't know, but now that I'm here, it'd be rude for me not to stay and eat."

"Yeah, right! You know better than I do when Auntie is cooking and I'm the one that lives here. But why are you knocking? Don't you have your keys? And where the hell were you yesterday? You forgot to pick me up!" I reply irritably.

Skye gasps, "Oh, my bad. I had so much going on yesterday that I completely forgot. Troy and I got into it and he took my keys. It's just been a bunch of drama."

Both curious, and concerned, I ask, "What you mean he took your keys? Why? Did you get them back?"

Skye smacks her lips and rolls her eyes. "Would I be knocking if I had my keys? Don't worry, I'll get them. He's just tripping right now."

"You better! I don't like the idea of him having access to me and Auntie," I say, feeling disturbed.

"I'm sure y'all are the last thing on Troy's mind. Both his house and car keys that he gave me are on the same ring. He's just trying to feel powerful by inconveniencing me." Skye nonchalantly walks to the kitchen. "Good morning, Auntie."

"Skye! What a pleasant surprise. I'm happy you came for breakfast." Aunt Jewel is already making Skye a plate.

"Me too, Auntie. Everything smells so good!"

"Sure does," I agree.

We sit at the small round table together and bow our heads to pray.

Aunt Jewel looks at Skye. "Will Troy be joining us?"

"No, he had some errands to run this morning."

I roll my eyes and scoff, "Errands? Is that what he calls it?"

"Stormey, don't start," Aunt Jewel warns.

"Stormey, seriously, what's your deal? Why are you always harping on Troy? What he does has nothing to do with you," Skye snaps.

"Well, to simply put it, Skye, I don't like him."

"You don't even know him. What is there for you to dislike?" Skye's annoyance is clear.

"I don't like how he disrespects you and tries to control you. Today is a prime example. You don't even have your own keys."

"Skye, what is she talking about?" Aunt Jewel inquires.

"It's really nothing, Auntie. It's not as big of a deal as she's trying to make it sound," Skye casually brushes off the question.

"It is that serious Auntie. She just doesn't want you to know," I quip.

"*Girl*, get some business. Clearly, you're bored. That's why you're always being so darn dramatic!"

"Troy is a danger to you in more than one way and just because you can't see the danger does not mean it doesn't exist," I reply.

"Stormey, I'm going to have to ask you to go to your room if you can't behave," Aunt Jewel interjects.

"Go to my room? For telling the truth?" I'm bewildered.

"Just because you think a thought doesn't make it true and your truth isn't everyone else's. Besides, this is not how we treat our guests. So, end this," Aunt Jewel demands.

"Stormey, I'm getting tired of your negative comments. I'm happy. Why can't you just be happy for me? Troy and I are fine. He takes good care of me. I don't want for anything and I will not apologize for it. You need to stop being so jealous."

"Jealous?" My mouth drops open. "Are you being serious right now? How could I ever be jealous of you?"

"Stormey!" Aunt Jewels slams her fork down on her plate.

"You are jealous, Stormey. I'm doing better and living better than you all while your life remains stagnant because you're afraid of your own shadow. You *choose* to stay here, stuck. Still here snuggling up under Auntie like you ain't grown already. You can have it all too, just like me, whenever you decide to stop being afraid to live," Skye snaps.

"Are you stupid? Is this how you really think or are you under some kind of spell? Is Troy drugging you, too?" I ask sarcastically.

"Stormey! That's enough! Go to you room!" Aunt Jewels demands.

Skye snaps back. "Drugs? Oh, now you're trying to be funny? And no, I'm not the one under a spell. You need to get out of your fantasy land and join the rest of us in the real world. You're a grown woman and it's time to get with the program. I mean, look at you. You're beautiful. Do you know how many men would love to have you as their arm candy? How much they'd give? We weren't born with these looks in vain. It's our meal ticket. We should never have to want for anything.

"You need to stop being so jealous of me and pull yourself together," Skye continues. "It's time to get a boyfriend. One with some money. He needs to be able to buy you things you never had, take you places you never been, and show you things you never seen. That, right there between your legs, is your pocketbook. It's not called that for nothing. No one is allowed to deposit there without depositing cash-in-your-hand. I don't understand why you're so mad about me doing exactly what we always said we'd do. I'm living the life we used to stay up at night and fantasize about!"

"No, you're not! You're doing the exact opposite!" Caught up in the moment of intensity, I ignore Aunt Jewel. "We said we'd never let a man use us up for his satisfaction. We said we'd wait on love and have our children with quality men who would be good fathers. I want to be in love with someone who is in love with me. To have sex for money, regardless of if you're advertising outside on the corner or not, is no better than what mother is doing and we both said we'd never be anything like her. But as it seems you are turning out to be just like her. Well, I can't join you.

"I'm saving myself for the right person." I continue, "Because laying with dogs like Troy will have you coming up with more than fleas. You signed a deal with the devil for shelter and material possessions, hugging and kissing on him to fulfill your wish list. The way I see it, there will come a day when you're going to be wishing you would've been more like me."

Skye chuckles sarcastically, "Be like you? You're delusional. And for your information, I'm *nothing* like mother. She's a junkie. She stands outside waiting to be picked up for pennies to support her addiction. Don't you ever compare me to her again! I'm *well* taken care of and have everything I want. I'll never be without again. You're walking around here talking about love and finding the one. Hell, you sound like you've been watching one too many Disney movies."

Skye continues, "Fairy tales don't exist in real life. Only foolish little girls lay on their backs in the name of love. Having sex with some guy because he makes you feel butterflies and giggle is worthless. What are you going to do when he decides he's done with you and wants someone else? He'll leave you sitting there with a used vagina, a broken heart, and empty pockets. You can have that! That'll never be me. A real woman won't let a man even think about touching her before receiving her gifts up front. The man that invests in you stays with you, and if he doesn't, then at least for the time and sex you spent you'll have your bills paid and some cute shoes to walk away in."

I'm disgusted. "You used to feel the same way I do. You've changed. All you care about is money, who has it, and how you can get it. Where did your morals go?"

Skye doesn't even take time to think about my question. "You're still talking about what we said when we were little girls. Those days are gone forever. Look at your life, Stormey. You can't live with Momma, her life is in shambles. You can't support yourself off the little bit of money you're making at the diner. And I hope you don't think you're going to live with Auntie forever. I mean seriously, what are you going to do? It's time for you to stop living in dreamland world and get a real plan."

"Is that your plan?" I ask. "To sleep with whomever has the most? Ha! How could I ever be jealous of you when I pity you? I thought I knew you, but now it's clear, I don't."

Skye snaps, "No, I pity you because you'll have to get your heart broken before you accept the world as it is. And if you think I'm still a foolish little girl living in a fantasy waiting on Price Charming, then you're right, you don't know me. I'm a grown woman now. I am not the same Skye anymore."

"It's taken me some time but I'm starting to see that now," I say quietly.

Finally, there's a moment of silence. Aunt Jewel, visibly upset, speaks. "Are you two finished? You two don't have to agree, but speaking to each other with disrespect is unacceptable. If you two can't do better, then it's best to not even be around each other until you can get over yourselves."

"I apologize, Auntie. I was so taken aback and engrossed in my anger, I couldn't hear you." I say remorsefully. I realize the girl I'm looking at isn't who I remember her to be. She's become a figment of my imagination. I don't know what has happened to her and I'm about to explode.

"I'm going to my room," I excuse myself from the table.

At the same time, Skye stands up. "I'm leaving too. Thank you for breakfast, Auntie." She gives Aunt Jewel a kiss on the cheek, "I'll let myself out."

Aunt Jewel comes into my room shortly after and finds me defacing the portrait I painted of Skye.

"Stormey, what has gotten into you? Why are you so angry?"

"I'm not angry! I'm not angry at all."

"Look at what you're doing and tell me you're not."

I take a step back, feeling the fire-like heat rush through my body. "Okay, so what? I'm angry! Wouldn't you be?"

"But I want to know why? Why does your sister get under your skin?"

I sit on the edge of my bed. "When it was just the two of us, things were different. She was different. We used to be so close and endured so much together. I thought it would always be us against the world, but now all she cares about is herself."

"I understand you miss your sister but you seem so unhappy. Are you unhappy?"

"I just feel forgotten and alone. I mean, I know I have you, but it's different. You weren't there. You don't understand me the way she does."

"But you're not there now so why are you insisting on her remaining the same when you're not even the same anymore either. How does that make things any better for you?"

"I don't know Auntie. I never really thought about it. I Just liked the idea of her always being here with me."

"Stormey, nothing, person or circumstance, stays the same forever. It's an unrealistic expectation and you will forever be disappointed if you can't accept that the only constant in life is change itself."

"I just want things to go back to the way they were. Do you think I'm being selfish?"

"It's not that you're being selfish, you're just not upset for the reasons you believe," she remarks.

"Well, then why am I upset?"

"You said you feel forgotten and alone. But why? You act as if your sister moving on somehow keeps you tied to the past alone. Why not move on too? Why do you dwell on memories that are long over? How is staying consumed with past trauma serving you, or better yet, how is it helping you to achieve your dreams? Do you believe that Amber's absence and Skye's leaving says something about you? Do you believe you're unlovable and unworthy because they became consumed in their own lives and didn't stick around for you? Help me understand what you're thinking and feeling."

"It doesn't mean anything about me, it means something about them!"

"Well, it may feel good to say it but do you really believe it? How does thinking about what was and what wasn't make anything better for you now?"

"I don't know," I respond.

"You *do* know," she rebuttals.

I think for a moment, then I mumble, "It doesn't."

"No, Stormey, it doesn't. Are any of the things you're so upset about, happening to you right now?"

"No," I reply.

"Exactly, it's happening in your mind and nowhere else," she says. "You don't need to suffer like this. You need to stop thinking thoughts that hurt you and replace them with thoughts that inspire you."

"But these things happened. It's not like I'm making it up," I reply.

"What happened to you is real but the point is, it's no longer happening. You're repeatedly playing the reruns through your mind, allowing yourself to be a prisoner to yourself," she explains.

"Well, how do I stop thinking about it? How do I forget things that hurt me?"

She replies, "It's not that you forget it. You understand it. Your mother didn't give you much, but she gave you everything she had. It wasn't because you weren't deserving of more, she just couldn't give you what she didn't have to give."

"Why was that all she had to give? Why couldn't she do more or be a better mother? Why do you always make excuses for her?"

"Your mother has her own story and it is not mine to tell. What I can tell you is that your mother was already fighting against her traumas before you or your sister came into this world. She tried fixing herself the best way she knew and made some poor choices that left her in the state she's in. But even in that state, she gave you her best. And when it comes to Skye, she's trying to find her way. I'm not saying she is making the best choices, but this is the first time she's experienced life this way. She's afraid of not having enough and is willing to do some things you're not, in order to have what she wants. She may come around and she may not but you have to let go of your judgments and expectations of her and begin to focus on yourself," she continues.

I ask, "What do you mean focus on myself? I'm fine. I'm not the one running in the streets."

"Stormey, you're focused on the wrong things. Happiness doesn't come from anyone or anything outside of you. It has to already be inside of you. If you don't bring your own happiness then it doesn't matter what happens in your life, you'll never feel it. Waiting on people or things to be a certain way before being able to be happy is setting yourself into an endless cycle where you're continuously looking for the next temporary fix.

"It's like being on drugs. Once the feeling leaves, you'll be off to the next thing until you learn you already have the power within to build and pump yourself up no matter what is happening around you. Don't look to others to give you the love, support, and encouragement you need, or else you'll always be disappointed. You have to be your own number one supporter and encourager. Be your own best friend."

"What do you mean, give it to myself? How?"

She reaches her hand out to me and says, "Come here. Let me show you."

I take her hand as she walks me to the mirror. She turns me around to see my own reflection.

"Acknowledge, praise, and affirm yourself. Think about everything you've ever hoped to hear from your mother, sister, father, or anyone else. Look into your own eyes and tell it to yourself. Say, "Good morning beautiful. I love you.""

"What? I'm not saying that. That's weird!"

"Stormey, you say you want to be more like me. If you want to be confident and unbothered by the trials of life then this is how you do it. You learn how to validate and approve of yourself before you walk out of this room each and every day.

Look at your face and smile. Remind yourself that you are worthy, worth it, and worthwhile. You are loved and lovable. You are whole, complete, and perfect as you are. You are safe and protected. You are the pot of gold at the end of the rainbow. You are the reason for the rainbow. You are blessed, favored, intelligent, and gifted. You are deserving of more than enough. Because you were given life, there is a divine purpose for your life."

She turns my head toward her, looks me in the eyes lovingly, and says, "The world is waiting on you to realize who you are. There is no limit to what you can do and where you can go. You're destined to have everything you can dream. All you have to do is show up full of belief in yourself and do what God has created you to do.

"You cannot change how your life began, but in this moment, you can begin to create the ending you envision. As change happens, remember to always love yourself through each lesson you must learn."

She turns my head back to the mirror and guides me through the affirmations again. I begin to giggle, looking into the mirror, attempting to repeat what she's saying.

Aunt Jewel stands behind me as she looks at my reflection. "Your power is in your mind. Whatever you believe about yourself and life will determine how you experience it. If you want to experience true joy, this is where you start. Remind yourself, who you are."

Aunt Jewel embraces me tightly. "I want you to continue speaking to yourself this way. Write these words down as often as you can until they are your own natural thoughts. Fight through the discomfort because eventually you won't accept anything less from yourself or anyone else."

She continues to stand next to me as I say it over again. At first, I feel a little weird but after the third or fourth time, it feels good to hear the words, to think those things are true. Maybe my life does have purpose. The mere fact I was born to a crack addict and have no physical defects nor mental disabilities is nothing short of a miracle. Maybe God did will my existence. Maybe He didn't neglect me after all. As I think about things differently, the internal gnawing pains begin to subside. Maybe it's true, my perspective matters more than I know.

CHAPTER 6

Reluctant

"Skye!" My shrill voice carries me out of my bedroom and into Skye's old bedroom. She spent the night but instead of worrying about why, I'm focused on me for once. I grab her shoulders to get her attention. "Remember the guy I told you I met at the diner?"

"Yeah, what about him?" Skye replies.

"Well, I'm going out with him tonight!"

"Girl! It's about time!"

"I knew you'd be excited, but I need a favor."

"What's up?"

"I'm a little nervous to go alone and so I asked him to bring his friend so that you could come with me. But I totally didn't consider Troy."

"Wait, what about Troy?"

"I'm sure he would be upset if you went out with another guy even if it is nothing."

"We're not married. Besides I want to go. I think it'll be fun," she answers.

"Okay! I wasn't trying to cause any problems but I'm super excited!"

"Girl, anything to get you out of this house, especially if it's with a man," Skye chuckles.

"We're going to have so much fun!" I jump up and down and hold onto her shoulders.

"Too excited," Skye laughs and pulls away.

"I'm going to tell Auntie," I skip away. Aunt Jewel is in her room laying on the bed reading her bible. "You're not going to believe this Auntie." I bait her but she doesn't take it quick enough. "I'm going on a date!"

"That's great, Stormey. Who's the lucky young man? I haven't heard you mention anyone lately."

"His name's Ace. He comes to the diner often. It's going to be a double date because Skye's coming too."

"That sounds like fun," she smiles.

"I know right! We're about to get dressed but I just wanted you to know."

"Okay but make sure you share your location with me so I know where you guys are," she requests.

"I will." I walk into my room and sit down on the bed, suddenly nervous about this date. What if I don't like him? What if he expects me to kiss him? What if he turns out to be a jerk? Okay, I gotta chill because I'm about to think myself out of going. It's been a while since Skye and I hung out and had fun together. That alone, makes it worthwhile.

"What are you doing? You should be getting dressed." Skye stands in the doorway wearing her leather color block jacket with skinny jeans, heels, bangles, and large hoop earrings.

"I *am* dressed."

"No, you're not. I won't let you go out embarrassing either one of us looking like Plain Jane. You'll never get a boyfriend like that." Skye rifles through my clothes and hands me a pair of skinny jeans, a plain shirt, and a black leather jacket. "Do you have any black heels?"

"Yeah, they're in the closet," I answer.

"Good. Put them on with that. And hurry up!" She calls over her shoulder as she walks out.

I get dressed and when I come out I look both of us over. "You do realize that you just dressed me to look like you."

"Of course! I keep a man. Take notes," she scoffs.

The doorbell echoes from downstairs and Skye struts to open it. To my surprise Ace is standing at the door holding a bouquet of flowers.

"Are those for me?" She asks.

He softly replies, "These are...umm...for Stormey."

"Where are mine?"

"I'm not sure. Maybe your date has yours," Ace awkwardly responds.

"Are you going to let him in?" Aunt Jewel walks into the room. Skye steps aside and waves her arm for him to enter.

"Good evening. Thanks for inviting me into your home. My name's Ace." He holds his hand out to greet Aunt Jewel.

"I see someone taught you well, young man. Which of my nieces are you here to see?"

Ace replies, "My friend Tyshawn and I will be escorting both ladies tonight."

She looks around. "Well, where is he?"

"He's still in the car. He received a phone call he needed to take just as we were pulling up."

Aunt Jewel asks, "Well, which of my nieces are you here for?"

Ace looks at me with a gentle smile and says, "I'm here for Stormey."

I begin to blush and grab my coat.

"Let me help you with that." He lays the flowers on the coffee table to assist me with my coat.

"Thank you."

He picks the flowers back up and hands them to me. "These are yours."

"Sunflowers," I reply with a smile. "Love them! These are my favorite."

"Really? I wanted to get something different than roses and when I saw these I thought they were uniquely beautiful like you."

"How kind of you to say that." I blush again and savor the fragrance.

"Oh okay, mister," Aunt Jewel gently takes the flowers from me. "I will put these in water for you."

Skye scowls, "Can we go now?"

Ace gestures to the door, looks at me, and says sweetly, "After you."

"Nice meeting you Ace," Aunt Jewel calls out.

"It was nice to meet you as well, ma'am," he responds.

We all walk to the car where Black is still inside talking on the phone. Ace opens the back door for me and the front door for Skye. He then walks to the other side of the car to get in next to me.

When Black finally hangs up the phone, Skye says, "So, you're my date, huh?"

"What's up Skye?" Black says.

"Y'all know each other?" I ask.

"Actually, we do. Where have you been girl?" Black asks.

"I've been around. Staying out of the way," Skye replies.

"I see that. You fell off the grid."

"Well, I guess tonight the universe conspired to help us make up for lost time," Skye says with a smile.

"Is that right?" Black smiles back.

We arrive at the Cinema Cafe where we have the option to either play pool, bowl, watch a movie, eat, or drink. Ace steps out of the car and opens my door. He puts his hand out and I put mine in his as he helps me out of the vehicle.

Skye yells out of the window, "We'll be in there in a minute. Y'all go ahead."

"Wait, what?" I respond confused.

"I want to talk to Black about something. We'll be right in," Skye assures me.

"Okay but don't take too long Skye," I warn.

Ace looks at me and says, "Shall we?"

"Sure, I guess," I say reluctantly. Upon entering I hear hip-hop music playing. Once inside there is a bar in the middle of the room, pool tables to the right, a bowling alley in the back, and a movie theatre to the left.

Ace asks, "So, what do you want to do?"

"Definitely not bowling. The last time I tried I accidentally threw my ball three lanes over and I'm not trying to hurt anybody today," I joke.

Ace laughs, "Okay, well, have you ever played pool before?"

"Nah."

He extends his arm for me to hold and I allow him to lead me to the pool tables. I send Skye a text letting her know we are playing pool. He places the balls in the rack and says, "This is how you properly rack. You have to make sure the ball with the number one on it is in the top of the triangle. The eight ball goes in the middle and one stripe and one solid in the bottom corners. Then you just fill the rest of the balls in, alternating every other one, stripe and solid."

"Okay." I pull out my phone to see that Skye replied, "I'm bowling with Black."

"You better pay attention because there will be a quiz later," he jokes.

"Yeah, right. You know I'm not going to remember this. Skye said she's over there bowling with Black." I scan the room trying to find her.

"Cool. Since you never played, I'll go first and show you how it's done." He hits the balls and they scatter all over the table. "You see how a striped ball fell into the side pocket? That means I have to sink all of the striped balls. You'll have the solids. Whoever hits all their balls in first then has to knock the eight ball in, and whoever does that, wins. Come over here so I can show you how to use your cue," he instructs.

"My what?"

"The stick in your hand. Let me show you how to use it." He smiles and I hesitantly walk over to him. "Are you right or left-handed?"

"Right." He places the small of the stick in between my fingers and the larger part in my right hand. Then he stands behind me and places his hand on the cue near mine. "Don't be getting all up on me now," I turn around and say.

He smiles, "Never. I'm a gentleman. I'm just trying to show you how to properly hit. I promise."

He stands behind me and moves the stick back and forth. "You see, you move the stick like this and push with your back hand. Go ahead and aim this white ball at one of your solid balls and try to knock it in."

I hit the white ball and it bounces on the table. Ace chuckles, "That's okay. Here, try it again, but aim for the middle of the ball."

I try again and hit a ball but it doesn't go anywhere near the hole. He stands behind me again. "Get low with me and look at the balls on the table. Think about which way you need the ball to move. If you need it to move right, then you need to hit it slightly from the left. If you need it to go left, then you would need to hit it from the right. Look at the balls and see the angles between them. It's something like geometry. And don't hit so hard. You'll overshoot that way." He gestures toward the table.

"This is too much," I complain.

"You'll get it," he assures me. He stands behind me again, placing his hands on the pool stick on top of mine, and brushes against mine gently. A chill shoots through my body causing me to shiver.

"You okay?" he asks.

"Yes, I'm fine, just a little chilly," I say, trying to conceal that I'm slightly aroused.

He stares into my eyes as if he can see behind the shadows of my fears. He pushes my hair off my face and gives me a comforting smile. Then he proceeds to help me hit the remaining balls on the table. Eventually, I begin playing like a pro. Okay, that's an over-statement, but I'm playing well. As the evening progresses, I begin to feel more comfortable. I catch myself staring at him because somewhere in my soul, I know that meeting him wasn't an accident, seeing him again wasn't a coincidence, and being with him tonight was unavoidable.

It feels like our coming together was divinely orchestrated and everything that happened before has led me to him. I feel an over-whelming desire to kiss him, but he's on his best behavior and wouldn't dare. I quickly break eye contact and look to the side when he catches me staring at him.

"How did you get the name Ace? Were you named after some-one?"

"Indirectly I was."

"What do you mean by that?"

"Well, my father goes by the name, King. He always says, if the father is worth anything, then the son will be greater. He loves the card game Spades and said the card greater than a King is the Ace. Therefore, that's what he named me."

"Oh, that's kind of deep," I respond.

"How did you get the name Stormey?"

"My mother gave birth to me during a rainstorm. She said I de-livered myself before she could made it to the hospital. So, she named me Stormey."

"That's dope! So, what do you like to do?"

"I don't do much, to be honest. Outside of working at the diner, I'm pretty much a homebody."

"You have to do something for fun. What do you do to have a good time?"

"You first, tell me about yourself," I redirect our conversation.

"Well, I'm the only son. I have an older sister. I am a senior at Prestige University and I'm finishing my degree in Business Science. I work at my uncle's car wash and hope to become the owner some-day soon. Now, your turn. What do you like to do, Stormey?"

"Wow, Prestige University? That's an elite school. It costs a for-tune to go there," I say in awe. "How long have you worked at the car wash for your uncle?"

"I've worked there since I graduated high school. But enough about me," he answers.

"Well, I love to paint; it's my escape," I reply.

"What kind of things do you paint?"

"Mostly portraits. I try to express the story of each soul by capturing the emotions shown in the face. It's sort of like telling a story without words, a story everyone understands."

"How long have you been doing that?"

"As far back as I can remember. I started drawing as a child. It was something that helped me stay occupied and take my focus off things happening around me. Eventually, my drawings evolved. I painted on everything including my bedroom walls. In our mom's home, Skye and I shared a room where I painted a life-size portrait of the two of us on the wall. I'm even responsible for a few graffiti murals around town."

"Really? You have to show me where they are! I would love to see your work."

"Okay, we can do that."

"Do you just paint for yourself or do you see it taking you somewhere?"

"I would love to make a career of it. I recently started posting my artwork on social media, hoping to get noticed by people that may want to buy my paintings to display in their homes, offices, and communities."

"If you paint with as much passion as you speak about it, then I believe you will get everything you hope for," he says.

"What about you? What do you want to do?" I ask.

"Since I work at my uncle's carwash and he's teaching me the ropes of being an entrepreneur, we plan to expand and open several more locations. Outside of that, I don't really have time for anything else."

"Well, what do *you* do for fun?" I mimic him.

He smiles, "I'm a homebody like you. I don't do much. I work a lot just trying to make sure the business is right, which doesn't leave a lot of time for kicking it."

Skye barges in and loudly interrupts, "Are y'all lovebirds ready?"

"It seems like we just got here," I reply.

"Tell me about it. We lost track of time catching up," she answers.

"How do you even know Black," I ask.

"Girl, they are about to close, are you ready or not?" Skye ignores my question.

"Yeah, we're ready." I'm reluctant for my evening with Ace to end.

"It's getting cold out." Ace wraps my coat around me and opens the door as we all walk out together.

"Did you guys have a good time? You think y'all might want to go out again?" Skye asks.

"Yeah, we did," I look at Ace, attempting to gauge whether he feels the same but his face is blank.

When we arrive back at the house, Ace escorts me to the door. "Thank you for coming out with me tonight," he says.

"I had a good time."

"Maybe we can go out again sometime. You know, just the two of us," he suggests with an enticing smile.

"I'd like that," I blush.

"I'll call you," he slowly releases my hand.

"Okay, goodnight." I stand in the doorway, smiling as he walks away.

Behind him, Skye walks to her car. I had hoped to have girl talk and tell her about my experience. "You're not coming in?"

"No, I'll be back. I have to take care of something," she yells.

"Okay." I wave goodbye and walk inside. I'm elated with how my date went. At first, I was reluctant to go, but now I celebrate a small victory as I feel release. I've finally taken a step to emerge out of my shell and it wasn't as scary as I thought it'd be. Now, I'm ready to take another.

CHAPTER 7

Weighted

The cloudy, sunless sky creates a gloomy and somber vibration. I really dislike winter's throbbing chill, but I try to shake away the blues by listening to my favorite music as I get ready for my date with Ace. I'm excited to see him again.

I put on my soft peach sweater, favorite jeans that hug me in all the right places, and knee-high riding boots with gold accents. I look at my reflection in the mirror as I dab concealer under my eyes while masking other imperfections, then I add a soft peach blush on my cheeks with a matching lip gloss, and a stroke of mascara. My auntie taught me that the trick to wearing make-up is to look like you aren't wearing much, if any. Make-up is to enhance, not trans-form. I'm feeling myself as I admire my flawless glow. My only real concern is whether Ace is feeling me.

He's on his way and should arrive any minute. These past two months have been enchanting. Each date has been one surprise af-ter the other and I can't believe how lucky I am. Each day I pinch myself just to know it's real. Ace is the guy I'd hoped for but didn't believe existed. He's attractive, kind, supportive, and genuine.

As soon as I hear the soft sound of his engine outside I grab my coat and scurry out before he gets a chance to come to the door.

"I heard you pull up," I say.

"I didn't expect you to be ready," he smiles as he walks around to open the door for me.

I get inside and reply with sass. "Well, next time I'll make you wait twenty minutes since I know you're expecting it."

He walks back to the driver's side and I reach over to open his door from the inside.

"That was nice," he leans over to give me a kiss on the cheek.

"I saw it done in an old movie I watched with my auntie. Where are we going?" I ask.

"Now you know I'm not telling you," he chuckles.

"You're such a tease. You should know by now that I'm too anxious and impatient for surprises."

"I know, but I love to see the expressions on your face when you see the surprises."

As we approach our destination, Ace pulls into a curved driveway topped with gravel that leads to a quaint cottage. Together, we walk to the door hand in hand. He opens the wooden door allowing me to walk in first. Inside is surprisingly modern with a hostess sitting at the desk to greet us.

"Hello, you must be Ace," the hostess says.

"Yes, I know I'm a few minutes early. Do you need more time to set up?"

"No, we're ready for you. Follow me." The hostess leads us into a dimly lit private room. Soft classical music is playing in the background, creating a romantic ambiance. As we turn the corner we walk into a beautiful room. Two easels sit in the middle of the floor with stools placed in front of them. I scan the room and observe beautiful paintings covering the walls, but I can tell most were completed by amateurs.

"We have you two set up in here," the hostess says. "You can either use one of these pre-drawn canvases or feel free to create something original of your own. Your easels are set with everything you should need, but if you are missing anything, feel free to give me a shout. I'll be right out front," she adds.

"Will do. Thanks," Ace responds. The hostess exits the room, leaving us alone.

"We're the only ones here?" I question. "I heard about this place, but I thought you needed a large group in order to have a private session."

"You do, but I bought all the tickets for tonight so we could be alone. I wanted to see you do what you love, but it wouldn't be the same in a room full of strangers," Ace replies.

"How did I get so lucky?" I gush.

"I'm the lucky one. You're a treasure and don't even know it."

"I think that's the nicest compliment I've ever received."

"I haven't met any other woman like you. Most have been too busy posing on social media trying to seem like they are more than they are. But you're just yourself, which is different, and I feel lucky that you're here with me," he responds.

"Stop it. You're always making me blush. What are you going to paint?"

"I don't know yet. I was thinking about attempting to create a paint-by-numbers version of that one over there with the birds flying from the barren tree. What about you?" Ace smiles.

"You'll have to wait until I finish," I laugh while turning my easel away.

"I'm sure whatever you choose will be better than mine," Ace says.

"What made you choose that painting?"

"To be honest, it's kind of my mood. I envy how birds are so light and can just take flight without a care. Sometimes I wish I could do the same."

"Why can't you take flight, other than the obvious?" I release a lighthearted laugh.

"I just feel tied down with responsibilities," he studies the painting.

"What kind of responsibilities? You don't have any kids to worry about."

"People are depending on me to finish school with honors and become a successful businessman. I feel like my father is trying to relive his life and somehow right his wrongs through me. Some days it weighs heavy on my shoulders. I just wish I could live life my way."

"That does seem heavy. I'm sorry you're dealing with that. Have you tried talking to your father to tell him how you feel?"

"No one challenges the King," he answers as he rolls up his sleeves.

"Wow. I bet that can't be easy."

"It's hard to stay focused on school and work as hard as I do but I would hate to disappoint my family, so I push through."

"You're a good son. If you need to talk and get things off your chest I'm here."

"I appreciate that. What's your family like? Do you have a lot of support?"

"Nothing special," I mumble as I begin to mix several paint colors.

"I know you live with your aunt but what about your parents?" he asks.

"I don't talk to my mother, and I don't know my father."

"Sorry, I didn't know. I don't want to make you feel uncomfortable," he apologizes.

"It's nothing to be sorry about. It's not a sore spot for me. I've come to terms with the fact that my family isn't much of one."

"How do you come to terms with something like that? I couldn't imagine not talking to my mom or dad."

"If you ever met my mother then you'd know how easy it is *not* to speak to her. When I was younger, I used to dream that one day my dad would come rescue me. I'd lay awake at night imagining how he'd look. I'd picture him being tall, handsome, and professional. I used to fall asleep thinking about him every night. Eventually, enough years went by, the dream died, and the pain and disappointment of accepting he's never coming back went away. The thought of him probably not even knowing I exist became more tolerable to bear," I explain.

"Tolerable to bear," Ace repeats. "That's real. There's so much pain in life, but no matter how much there is, it's still tolerable. Life is always changing so much. I look on social media and see all the violence against men that look like me and feel like I'm damned if I do and damned if I don't. My father has done everything he can think of to keep me out of the streets, but as I watch the countless news stories I have to ask, does it really matter if I have a degree? I can be doing everything right and still become a victim to the color of my skin.

"Whoever created language was strategic in labeling dark with evil. No one's going to ask if I'm educated and degreed before labeling me a threat. People are not even conscious of the fact that they instinctively see me as one either. It's like I have to work extra hard just to put them at ease by speaking and dressing a particular way. I can't be too masculine, authoritative, or self-assured. I can't express my feelings or say I need a shoulder to lean on or reveal that I don't have it all figured out. The way the odds are stacked against a young black man from the hood, it feels like everything is designed for me to fail. I know failure isn't an option but I wish I didn't have to try to overcome society's roadblocks and judgments on the road to success."

"You can only be who you are." I select a new brush. "Going against your nature to conform to expectations will only cause you suffering in the end. So, everything you do matters."

"I hear you. I'm just expressing some of the thoughts that frequent my mind. Sometimes I just need to hear them out loud to sort everything out," Ace explains.

"I personally hate drugs, drug dealers, drug addicts, and everything of the sort."

"Why are you so passionate about that when you don't have to deal with it?"

"I've been dealing with the effects of drugs every day since the beginning of my existence. My mother's an addict," I state.

"I didn't know. I apologize for assuming. You just turned out so well. I would've never thought it," Ace replies as he dips his brush in blue paint.

"I know you didn't know. It's not one of those things that a person goes around advertising, like, "Hi, I'm Stormey and my mother is a crackhead whore, what's your name?"" I joke.

"No, I don't think you'd advertise it, I just thought something like that would've come up by now," Ace answers.

"Everything is revealed in due time and I know first-hand what drugs do to people and their families because I'm a product of it," I reply.

"What was that like?"

"We lived in an apartment building that should've been condemned. The slumlord refused to fix the ceilings that leaked and fell in on our heads, and he didn't clean the halls that smelled like beer and piss. He salivated at the mouth whenever he laid eyes on me and Skye and repeatedly offered to take us as payment for rent. It was a demeaning way to live. And that's not even the worst of it," I say.

"What's the worst of it?" Ace asks.

"I don't know why I mentioned it because I don't like talking about it."

"Well, I care about you and I'd like to know what you've been through in life, but I don't want to make you feel uncomfortable."

"It's a long story, but the short version is that the asshole slumlord tried to force himself on me but Jay came to my rescue before anything could happen."

"Wow, I'm so sorry. You didn't deserve to go through that."

"Tell me, does anyone deserve to go through that?"

"Well, no, actually, but not you especially."

"Some people are just plain sick in the head. To do something like that to anyone is evil."

"What did your mother say about it?"

"I never told her. It's her fault I had to go through any of it anyway," I answer.

"Do you and your mom have a relationship?" Ace asks.

"No, she's too screwed up. I used to ask her how she got so far gone. I wanted to know her first mistake, partly because I wanted to understand her and partly because I wanted to be sure to never repeat it. I could always tell that something haunted her mind. Trying to get her to open up has done nothing but push her deeper into her darkness. She never talks about her past and keeps herself so high that she hardly says anything at all.

"There were moments when she would butter me up and sweet talk my sister but I later realized it was just manipulation to get money from us so she could get her next fix. When we got hip and stopped playing along she would tweak out and yell, cursing us for being born and blaming our existence for her not having enough money to smoke the rest of her life away. Eventually, I stopped asking and caring. I just made up my mind to never be anything like her. In a way, she's become my motivation."

"Is she the motivation behind your paintings, too?" Ace asks.

"I wouldn't say that, but the circumstances she created pushed me to a place where I needed an outlet and I just so happened to have found it in painting."

"I think you're the first person I ever met that actually paints for real and not just as a hobby. No offense, I think it's dope, but it's different. Do you ever think about being anything else other than a painter?"

"People ask me all the time what I'm going to do if I don't make it. I don't understand that way of thinking or how to answer the question. I can capture what other people feel on a canvas. I see beyond their mask and into their souls. I'm an artist. God created each one of us with a purpose and a gift. Artistic expression is mine. How can anyone fail while doing what they're created to do? I don't paint because I seek to be the next Picasso. I do it because it soothes the cry of my soul."

I continue rambling on. When I finally take a breath, I notice Ace staring at me. His eyes are so endearing. Him looking at me makes me feel so warm inside. I never knew what it felt like to be revered and I can't help but look back at him with the same reverence.

"I'm done with my painting." Ace motions me over while still gazing into my eyes. "Come and look at it."

"That's actually pretty good. You're a natural," I compliment.

"You're kind, but this isn't good," he laughs.

"It is. I promise," I laugh with him.

"Are you done with yours or is it still a secret?" he asks.

"I'm pretty much finished. I was just adding details." I walk him over to my canvas.

"Wow! This is dope! I've never had anyone paint *me* before," he exclaims.

"Well, now you have. You make great art," I flirt.

He doesn't say a word as he gently places his hand on the back of my head and slides his fingers through my hair. Staring into my eyes, he leans in and presses his full, soft lips against mine. I close my eyes and let myself flow with what feels like a magnet pulling me into him. I've never had a real kiss before, but somehow, I know no other would compare.

He takes a step back and looks at me. Bashful, I turn my head to break our stare. He looks at the clock and says, "I have to get you home before it gets too late."

"I'm not ready," I moan.

"I'm not either, but I don't want your aunt to think bad of me."

"I know. That's why she loves you," I respond disappointedly. As he kisses me on the cheek, I can no longer feel the ground beneath my feet. His touch makes me feel like I'm floating on clouds.

CHAPTER 8

Hearts Turned Dark

It's just before midnight when I arrive at the diner. As I'm walking in, a tall, slender lady with a darker complexion pushes past me, heading toward the parking lot. "You messed with the wrong one this time," she yells out behind her.

Black runs out after her, "Ma, you gotta chill."

She twirls her arm in the air as she turns and walks away from him. "I'll chill when you run me my cash."

Black shakes and lowers his head as he hands her a wad of cash. Clearly irritated, he asks, "Are you happy now?"

She snatches the money and turns her back to him. As she walks away, she warns, "Next time don't make me come find you."

Black quietly walks back inside and sits at the table with King and Ace. He looks at Ace and asks, "What are you doing here?"

"He was with me when you called. It won't matter because we should be in and out," explains King.

"They're only expecting the two of us. He needs to go," Black explains while pointing to the door.

"I'm not going with y'all. I got something to do anyway," Ace answers. "But dude, what's up with your mom? Why is she always spazzing out like that?"

"Toya has always been off the chain," King interjects.

Ace repeats, "No seriously, what's up with that?"

Black sits silently clinching his jaws. "She ain't always spazzing. She just likes to show out when he's around." He nods his head towards King. "He ever tell you the story about how he used to date my mom before he got with your mom?"

"Your mother told you about that?" King appears surprised.

"Of course she told me," Black states.

"You used to date her? For real?" Ace looks over to King.

"What's that supposed to mean?" Black asks appearing offended.

"No disrespect. I'm just surprised this never came up before today," Ace replies.

King clears his throat and gestures toward Black. "Yeah, well I know you didn't call me here to talk about that so what's so urgent that you needed to meet in person?"

Black replies, "I got a new connect I want you to meet. If everything checks out then we will be able to expand our business internationally. This is a big deal and I really don't think I should go without you."

"You know I handle business during business hours. I spend my nights at home with my family," King reminds Black.

"Don't worry, it'll be quick."

"When I told you I'd start letting you make your own moves, that's what I meant. I'm not going to be out here holding your hand. On top of that, we don't need to go bigger, greed is the surest way to lose everything."

Black replies, "Trust me, I can handle it on my own. I just wanted you to hear for yourself. Opportunities like this don't come around often and should be given some real consideration."

King responds, "Everyone knows I don't do business with anyone that I don't already know. I don't care how good and rare this opportunity is because I'm not going. I don't make exceptions to my rules, not even for you."

"Damn. You're going to leave me hanging like that," Black replies with an angry stare.

King says, "Everything that glitters isn't gold."

Black replies, "This one is."

"You're so much like your mother it's scary," King shakes his head.

"Now you want to talk about my mother?" Black snaps.

"Watch it now," King warns.

Ace tries to break the tension. "You and mom been together over twenty years, was his mom your high school sweetheart or something?"

"Yeah, she was," King answers.

"Y'all barely speak now, did y'all break up on bad terms?" Ace inquires.

"Back in high school, Toya was a go-getter just like Black," King answers. "She was a street girl and had the hookup on practically everything. Everyone knew that anything they wanted, whether clothes, electronics, appliances, or whatever, they could get it from Toya. She had the best quality for the lowest price and if she didn't have it, she knew who did. She wore the most fly clothes and only drove foreign cars. She was that chick. When dope hit the streets we began hustling together, making thousands a day, which wasn't bad for beginners.

"Toya was fun, but she was demanding and consumed by material possessions. She only knew two ways to determine a person's worth and that was either by what they had or what they had on. There was no other criteria. I knew that if I wanted to keep her happy I'd always be under pressure to remain in the streets.

"Although Toya had been with me from the beginning, it was always understood that if I could no longer afford to maintain our image, she would move onto the next man that could."

I try to read Black's energy but he's quiet and expressionless as he listens.

"It's blowing my mind how you have so much history with my best friend's mom and never thought to say anything," Ace interrupts.

King replies, "Toya and I had an on and off again type of relationship and while we were off, I met your mom and we never got back on again. Toya was so used to me coming back that she never even considered that I had actually moved on until she learned that Diamond and I had gotten married. That's when I saw a different side of her and she hasn't really spoken to me since. I learned a valuable lesson from that experience."

"What's that?" Black asked, suddenly interested again.

"There's equal power in love and hate. A heart full of love and loyalty can carry you to the highest of heights, just as a heart full of hate and hurt can bring about your demise. When it's all said and done, my lifestyle is too dangerous to add the additional risk of playing with hearts turned dark."

"This is crazy," Ace says.

"Yeah. Crazy, right?" Black never looks up from his phone.

King says, "I've been thinking a lot lately about retiring. That's why I've been teaching you everything I know because you will soon be calling the shots. Consider it a rite of passage."

Black looks up from his phone and says, "Retire? For what? There's too much money to be made out here to be throwing in the towel."

"The irony of you telling Black not to expand, yet talking about stepping down at the same time," Ace says.

King states, "Yom Kippur is the holiest day of the year for the Jewish people. It's when they ask God to forgive them for all the wrongs they've done, then they throw breadcrumbs into water. As I understand it, they believe that doing so frees them from the guilt and responsibility of their sins. Other cultures have a similar practice using fire. They'll write their sins on a piece of paper and then toss the paper into burning flames. As the paper burns, they believe the same is true for their toxic traits."

Black, who's consumed with his phone, looks up again and in a condescending tone asks, "What are you talking about old man? You went from dark hearts to retiring to burning paper. Are you feeling okay?"

Ignoring Black's question, King continues, "Have you done anything you wished you could take back? Have you ever wronged someone you wished to un-wrong? Think about how much easier life would be if righting wrongs were as simple as throwing bread in water or paper in fire. The reality is, there are just some things you can never take back. No matter how bad you feel, some damage cannot be repaired."

Annoyed, Blacks asks, "Where are you going with this National Geographic speech?"

King responds, "Just life. Sometimes I wonder how I ended up here. This was not the life I thought I'd be living after forty. I thought I'd be done by now. I was supposed to be retired and traveling the world with my family. I'm not supposed to still be out here moving weight. This business turned me into someone I never thought I'd be, doing things I never thought I'd do. I've broken promises and hearts, including your mother's. I never meant to hurt her, but she still hates me. I wish I could throw some paper in a fire and have her forgive me. I learned hard lessons by hurting people I never foresaw hurting."

Black says, "If it happened the way you said then you didn't do anything wrong except fall for another woman when y'all weren't even together. It's not like you cheated or nothing."

"Have you ever sat back and wondered why you do what you do? Are you doing it because you want to or because it's your family's ritual?" King asks.

Black cockily replies, "I get money. That's my family's ritual."

King shakes his head, "That's my point."

"Well, I still have a meeting to go to." Black jumps up from his seat.

King sternly states, "I told you I'm not expanding."

"You're not. But as a matter of fact, I am." Black walks towards the door with King following behind.

Once outside, King warns, "Don't get beside yourself and in over your head. I'm not coming to save you if you do."

Suddenly, gun shots spew through the diner windows, shattering all the glass. My heart feels like it's bursting out of my chest. Terrified, I scream.

"Get down!" Ace runs toward me and rolls over the counter, pulling me down to the floor. After what feels like an eternity, the shots cease, but I remain shaking in Ace's arms. The door to the diner swings open and I tremble even harder.

"Shhhh." Ace holds me in his arms and pulls broken glass out of my hair. "Are you okay?"

"Yes," I whisper.

"Ace! Are you in here?" Black screams frantically.

Ace slowly stands up. "Where's my dad?"

Black, covered in blood, screams, "We were ambushed. King's been shot. Come on! We gotta get him to the hospital."

I hear groaning. Just outside the window, King lays on the ground in a pool of his own blood.

Ace runs to him, "Dad! I'm going to get you out of here!" King nods as he continues to groan in pain. "Black, help me carry him," Ace demands.

They both lift King from the ground, Ace holding him under his arms and Black carrying his feet. "Don't worry, Pops! You're going to be okay. Keep breathing. Just keep breathing."

They carry King to his truck and lay him in the back seat. Still in shock, I stare as they speed away. Reality sets in as I begin double checking myself to see if I've been shot or cut by glass. A feeling of relief takes over as I realize I'm not bleeding. My phone vibrates in my pocket. I look at the screen and see Skye is calling. "Hello?"

"Stormey, where are you?" Skye asks.

"I'm at the diner and you wouldn't believe…"

She cuts me off. "Aunt Jewel is in the hospital. I'm on my way to get you."

My heart drops upon hearing the news. "Please tell me she's okay. I don't think I can handle anything else tonight."

She replies, "All I know is that she was rushed to the emergency room. I'm pulling up. Come outside."

I see Troy's coupe pull up and I look around nervously as I hurry to get into the passenger side. Skye asks, "What the hell happened here?"

"Please just go!" I yell frantically.

Skye speeds off like a mad woman as she demands, "Stormey tell me what the hell happened back there!"

"I was at the counter and bullets…gunshots…blood…I don't know. Ace saved me." I stumble over my words as I try to explain.

"Who were they shooting at? Did anyone get shot?" Skye asks.

"Ace's dad got shot."

"They shot King?" Skye exclaims in disbelief.

"Yeah, but I don't feel like talking." I'm overwhelmed by everything that's happening. The only thing that could make this night worse is if we arrive at the hospital as patients ourselves because of Skye's reckless driving, but shock keeps me quiet.

CHAPTER 9

Same Room, Different Views

We arrive and quickly rush into the emergency room. I walk straight to the receptionist's desk. The words rush out my mouth in a panic. "My aunt, Jewel Knights, was brought here."

The receptionist politely replies, "She's in room nineteen but isn't allowed any visitors just yet. Have a seat in the waiting area. Someone will notify you when you can go back to see her."

Agitated, I ask, "Well, is everything okay? Why is she here, anyway?"

The receptionist replies, "I wish I could tell you, but you'll have to wait to talk with her doctor."

I don't want to wait. I hate not knowing what's going on but reluctantly, I reply, "Thank you."

"I'll get us something to drink from the vending machine," Skye walks off.

"Okay." I take a seat. I check the time on my phone for what seems like the hundredth time but it hasn't even been an hour. As thoughts race through my mind, it dawns on me that I never thought about Aunt Jewel getting sick before. I can't remember the last time I even saw her with a cold. As I begin to obsess over worst-case scenarios, I realize that I don't know what I'd do without her. Who will I have if I don't have her? I can't count on my mother because she can't even count on herself. And lately Skye is all about Skye. She's gotten a taste of the fast life and is on some mission to be taken care of by any random lowlife. I can't even count on her to get me a soda. She went to get my drink before I sat down and she still hasn't returned. She's probably somewhere trying to seduce a doctor.

I get up to find her. Walking through the waiting area, I scan the room. As an artist, I'm always examining the faces around me, trying to interpret their expressions. I can learn more about a person through their eyes than they could ever tell me through their mouth.

I can see who's here because they're not feeling well, their face reveals their discomfort. I see who's here for their loved ones because their eyes reveal worry and concern. Different people. Different races. Different economic classes. All gathered in the same room, united by fear. It's the fear you feel when you accept your humanness and understand what little power you have when it comes to life and death. It's the instant when you choose whether to run to God or to curse Him for allowing you to suffer. It's the moment when you find out how strong or weak you really are.

As I continue walking, I look up and I'm surprised to see Ace pacing. Back and forth. Forth and back. Staring at the ceiling as if he can see the answer to his prayers as they come down from the heavens. I don't mean to stare at him but he notices me before I can walk away. Our eyes lock for several seconds before I decide to walk over to him.

I grab his hand. "You're walking a hole in the floor. Have a seat with me."

"I can't sit still," he states. "I can't even think right now."

"Have you heard anything yet?" I ask.

"We're waiting for him to get out of surgery."

"I'm sorry this happened but it's a good sign that he made it to surgery."

"I hope so," he says with a look of worry on his face.

"You should think about what you are going to say to him when he gets out of surgery, it'll help you worry less."

"Maybe. Did you come to check on him?"

"My aunt was rushed to the hospital too, so I'm waiting on permission to see her."

"Listen to your girl." Black stands calmly against the wall with his head leaned back. To my surprise, Skye is standing in front of him, her head to the side, breasts poked out, smile wide. "Pacing won't make his surgery go any better. So, why don't you calm down and have a seat?"

Ace snaps angrily, "Calm down? What do you mean calm down? My father is fighting for his life! Matter of fact, why are you so calm? You could have been shot too. We all could've been. How can you stand here like nothing's going on?"

"Either you are going to pray or worry, but you can't do both at the same time. If I were your imaginary God, I'd be insulted."

"Imaginary?" Ace responds. "You should be thanking God that you aren't in the operating room next to him."

Black retaliates, "You're acting like someone who doesn't trust in what you say you believe. Either you believe God will bring him through or you don't. So, please sit down."

Ace's jaws tighten, and his back teeth begin to grind. "If I were you, I'd stop talking right now. I would get angry, but you don't even have a father, so you could never understand what I'm going through."

The doctor comes out and Ace runs to him. "Sir, your father's surgery went well. He's awake now and you may see him."

Ace exhales a heavy sigh of relief. The anxiety and fear visibly leave his body. He quickly follows the doctor through the double doors that separate the waiting room from the private area. Black slowly follows behind.

Skye notices me and calls out, "Stormey, come here!"

I walk over and sarcastically ask, "Did you forget something?"

"My bad. I forgot that fast," she replies.

"That's obvious," I glare at her angrily. "No one came out to get us yet so I'm going to check again."

When I arrive at the receptionist's desk she is on the phone. "Excuse me, I've been waiting to hear something about Jewel Knights. When will we be able to see her?"

"Hold on one minute," she looks on her computer for an update. "You can see her now. She's in room nineteen. Go through those doors, turn right, and follow the hall, you will see the sign."

"Thank you," I scurry off to find her. I arrive right as the doctor is exiting. "Doctor, my aunt is in there. Is she okay?"

He replies, "I can't tell you much except that we are running some tests. She will be able to fill you in."

"Thank you." I enter the room and see her lying in bed with her eyes closed. She has a breathing tube through her nose and the monitor beeps with her pulse. She's always been Super Woman, but I see her mortality for the first time. She just doesn't look like herself. I sit down and stare at her in disbelief, watching her sleep.

Skye enters the room and asks, "What did they say is wrong with her?"

"They haven't said anything yet."

Skye replies, "Did you see Black, though? He dresses like understated money."

"What does that even mean?"

She looks at me to see if I'm serious. "It means he has money. Real money. He wears labels not to impress others, but because that's just what he wears. Quality. The average person wouldn't even know what he's wearing, but I got the eye."

"Oh, here you go." I sigh and roll my eyes.

"Let me school you. See, you have to beware of the overstated labels. The ones that wear it to be seen are the ones that want to look like money but have none. I call them Great Pretenders. Don't fall for that."

I wonder what makes her think I care, especially at a time like this. I whisper, "Aunt Jewel is waking up." I hope she wasn't listening to us. She must've felt our presence in the room because she opened her eyes and smiled glowingly.

I immediately get up to kiss her on the forehead and gush, "I'm so happy you're awake. I was so worried. How are you feeling?"

Skye asks, "Aunt Jewel, what happened?""

She replies, "I felt a little overheated, but I ignored it and kept working around the house. The next thing I knew I was here. I guess I've been pushing myself too hard lately. I just need to rest a bit. I'll be fine."

"You scared the life out of us!" Skye exclaims. We both still have questions but before we can finish, our mother enters the room. She and Aunt Jewel are fourteen months apart in age but my mother looks twenty years older. Aunt Jewel says they were extremely close growing up but I don't understand how they turned out to be complete opposites. Night and day, good and evil, heaven and hell, and anything else that explains polar opposites. It's hard to believe they came from the same womb and it's unimaginable that they were raised in the same home.

Aunt Jewel embodies everything that being a woman is about. She exudes wisdom just in the way she walks. Sometimes I learn just from being in her presence. Whenever I remind her of her beauty she says, "A woman's strength comes from within. Physical beauty can only get you to the door. It's the mind that will open it and there's nothing that a beautiful woman with a strong mind cannot accomplish."

Aunt Jewel is everything I aspire to be while my so-called-mother is everything I despise. I refuse to make eye contact with her, let alone speak. She looks like she bathed recently but it doesn't matter how much soap she uses, she'll never be able to wash away the sins of being a horrible mother.

She hugs Aunt Jewel and says, "I came as soon as I heard."

Surprised, Aunt Jewel asks, "How did you know I was here?"

Amber replies, "Skye told me."

"Where have you been? No one has heard from you?" Aunt Jewel asks.

"I've been staying out the way. You know I've been clean for three days now!" Amber gloats.

I sigh and roll my eyes. Three whole days. What a joke! Who does she think she's fooling? I bet she's never been clean for three minutes. I glare at Skye and mumble, "I can't believe you called her."

Skye smacks her lips and says, "It's her sister. She deserves to know."

I start in on my mother, "Why are you lying? I just saw you out there tricking a few days ago. Now, after all these years, you expect us to believe that you've suddenly seen the light and want to be clean? Get out of here. No one even wants you here."

Aunt Jewel turns to me, "Stormey, that is no way to speak to your mother!"

With a face of stone, I ask, "What mother?"

Aunt Jewel says, "Stormey, I taught you better. You will not be disrespectful in my presence. She is, and will always be your mother. That won't change."

"She's an egg donor, yes, but a mother? No. She has not earned that title."

Amber says, "You can say what you want but like it or not, I am still your mother and God is watching."

I try my best to hold my tongue, but it's a failed effort. "Look at you standing over there all full of yourself, talking about God watching me as if he isn't watching you. You're pathetic. How can you call yourself a mother? Who have you mothered? Yes, you gave birth to us, but it stopped there. What have you done for me? Ever? The only thing I remember about you are your dazed eyes, the countless strange men, and everything Skye and I needed to survive, disappearing piece by piece. I don't know my father and I wish I didn't know you."

Amber angrily responds, "You think you're better than me? You think you're something, huh? You know so much about life. Poor

Stormey had it so bad. You don't know squat and you don't have a clue of how bad it really can get!"

"You used to say you got high to escape the pain, but the pain of what? All I see is self-inflicted misery. No one is forcing you to do drugs or to lay with strange men for nickels and dimes. It doesn't make sense and I will never respect you."

I stop myself from speaking any further. I know I've already said too much, but at the same time, it feels good to say it. I know Aunt Jewel is disappointed, but if the truth is too much for Amber to handle, then she should change what she's doing. But I won't say anymore. I don't want to give her the pleasure of using my words as fuel to flame her pipe.

Aunt Jewel raises her voice. "Stormey, who taught you to be so unforgiving? Apologize to your mother right now. I don't know what has gotten into you, but I will not tolerate it. You're not perfect, no one is. You cannot judge someone because their mess shows up differently than yours. Each of us have made mistakes that hurt or let down someone else, whether intentional or not. God has commanded you to honor your parents and what you are doing is far from that. I'm beyond disappointed with your attitude right now!"

Irritated, I respond, "Aunt Jewel, I love you, but I need to get out of here."

As I walk out of the room, Amber attempts to grab my arm. I snatch it away and tell her, "If you touch me you'll be lucky to already be in a hospital."

I storm out of the room into the hall. The nerve of that woman calling herself my mother. In the next room I hear a man say, "Wipe those goddamn tears from your eyes. Crying is for punks."

"What do you mean? Look at you! Who did this to you?" Responds a familiar voice. It's Ace.

I move closer so I can hear. King says, "I need you to man up, Son. There's something I need to say to you."

"No, Dad. Save your energy," Ace pleads.

King says, "Listen to me, Ace, this is important. I know I haven't always been there. I did a lot of wrong by you and your mother but you are becoming a man and you'll see that things aren't as cut and dry as you think. Taking care of a family isn't easy and there are a lot of tough decisions to be made. You will do things you said you would never do in order to keep food on the table and smiles on the faces of the ones you love."

I hear him take a breath through the oxygen mask. He continues, "I'm not saying this justifies anything, because I know I will burn in the furnace for all I've done. I'm just saying that one day you will understand. I stayed in this game past my expiration date. I was supposed to leave on my own terms, but greed wouldn't let me stop. I knew I was living in a dark world and I knew what I was doing wasn't right, but the lure of having nice things and money overrode everything else.

"I fell victim to the illusion that having money made me invincible. Money made me lovable, and everyone worshipped me. It gave me power; I was the King. These snakes should've never been able to get this close to me."

King pauses to take a long pause to breathe more oxygen into his lungs. "People relied on me to take care of them and I spent my days living up to the expectations of others and their perception of who I was until it became my image. I kept up the facade so I wouldn't let anyone down. And I never slowed down to see how much time was passing by. It's been exhausting to wear this mask and I've been too tired for too long.

"This right here, is my wake-up call. I'm done chasing illusions. You, son, you are my heir, my legacy. You are the Ace and have no other choice than to be better than the King. Tell your mother I love her and I'm sorry. Take good care of her and your sister. They deserve it."

"Why are you talking like you're dying? Your surgery went well. You can tell them yourself when they get here," Ace states.

King takes another long pause. "Whoever did this knows better than to leave the job undone. It's not over until they get what they want."

"And what is it that they want?" Ace questions.

King states, "My seat on the throne. You and Black are going to need each other more than ever now. I know you guys have been each other's closest friends since as far back as you can remember, but you are more than that. You guys are brothers."

Ace responds, "You already know he couldn't be any more of my brother if we shared the same blood."

King reiterates, "Son, he already does. He *is* my son and he *is* your brother."

Black's voice cracks as he says, "This is what it takes for you to finally acknowledge me? For years I've waited for this moment."

Startled by his response, King asks, "You knew?"

"You think I didn't? You think it was by coincidence that I came into your life?" Black answers.

"Why didn't you say anything?" King questions.

"Why didn't you?" Black retorts.

Now grimacing, Black, no longer afraid to speak up, continues, "My mother told me you agreed to always take care of us as long as she kept your secret, me. She told me that we could never admit our relationship because it would ruin your family, but I was your family. Ace became a brother to me but when I befriended him it was only to get closer to you. I wanted to know what it would be like to have you in my life. I watched you treat my mother like she was a mistake while you treated his like a queen. I watched you and Ace interact at his birthday parties. I watched you go to all his ball games, screaming his name only, even though we played on the same team. I watched you buy him a car when he turned sixteen, while I worked for you to earn the money to buy what I wanted or needed.

"On prom night, Ace and I rode in the same limo and again, I watched you embrace him and give him advice on how to be a gentleman with his date, when all you said to me was to have a good time. I watched you tell him how proud you were of him at graduation and how he was going to accomplish great things. I stood by and watched the whole time wishing it was me.

"I ran the streets with you, learned the game with you, and became your most loyal lieutenant to prove myself worthy of you, all while masquerading my pain and enduring more than anyone should have to bear. Still, I smiled, but behind it I yearned for you to see me, to acknowledge me as your own, to be good enough to be called your son.

"I dreamed of the day where you would find out that I was Toya's son and then you would know I was your son, too. But to my surprise you already knew who I was, so that day never came. I was plagued with questions every day. Do I count? Do I matter? Why couldn't you see me? Through it all I still loved you, remained loyal to you, and still, I hoped. Now, on this bed, when you have nothing to lose, you finally acknowledge me. I looked up to you. I believed in you and your code of honor. Now I see you are a nothing but a coward but even in this moment, I still love you. But I don't need you because you never wanted me."

King breathes slowly. "You've always exuded darkness and I could never figure out why. I called you Black because of it. I blamed your mother for not raising you right. I kept you near me because I thought I could teach you better than her. I thought if you learned how I thought, then you would grow up to be a strong businessman, but I could never pull you out of your darkness. I never realized that I was the overcast in your life. You didn't need street knowledge; you needed a father's guidance. I neglected you and it was for my own selfish reasons, but it was never because I thought you were insignificant. I just couldn't recognize how significant it was for you to have me."

I continue standing outside the room in disbelief. I can only imagine what Ace is feeling right now. Ace breaks his silence and interjects, "The two people I love have been lying to me my whole life? I trusted you, but you both betrayed me. The father that taught me about being a man and the importance of family has been nothing more than a hypocrite! The friend that I shared secrets with, opened up to, and loved as a brother, really was my brother? And you knew it? Here I thought we were friends but you used me to get near him. Among the three of us, our friendship, our relationship, and our bond have all been built on nothing more than lies. Like father like son. You two deserve each other."

I hear swift footsteps coming towards me, so I run to hide behind the curtain as I see Ace storm out the room.

"Ace!" King struggles to yell.

Enraged and overwhelmed with emotions, Ace punches the wall in the hallway. I can still hear Black and King talking inside.

Black says, "I waited my whole life for you to acknowledge me as your son, to be embraced by Ace as my brother, for the day I would be a part of your family, to hear you apologize. Now that the day has arrived, it doesn't feel how I thought it would. Nothing is different. The pain isn't gone. You waited too long to save me."

The room is quiet until I hear King gasp for air, the machine monitoring his now one long high-pitched beep. Ace hurries back into the room.

"What happened?" Ace asks. Black remains silent. The nurses run past me and enter the room. Ace walks backwards slowly out of the room. Black is walking quicker to catch up to him.

"You knew? You never thought one day to say, "Hey, I'm your brother?"" Ace yells.

Black counters, "I played my role so my mother would be taken care of. I did as I was told."

The doctor walks toward them with a solemn look on his face, "Your father went into cardiac shock. We tried all that we could, but we were unable to save him."

Ace goes silent. The room grows taller as he slowly drops to the floor, landing on his knees. Hot tears slide down his face. He speaks softly, "I was just talking to him. He seemed fine. Maybe I shouldn't have stormed out on him. Maybe it was too much for him to take."

Black kneels next to him and places his hand on Ace's back and says, "We will get through this together, brother."

Ace's tears appear to dry instantaneously. His fingers clinch tightly into fists. His grief turns into rage at the sound of Black's voice. Without acknowledging him, Ace rises slowly and walks towards the exit.

"Ace, where are you going?" Black calls out.

I watch as Ace keeps walking without looking back.

"Stormey! Girl, what has gotten into you? You went too far in there!" Skye yells as she points to Aunt Jewel's room, down the hall.

I say sarcastically, "I don't think I went far enough. I don't know what you were thinking when you called her. What makes you think she has the right to know about anything that's going on with any of us?"

Skye answers, "Regardless of what she did or didn't do, she's still our mother and she has the right to know if her sister is ill. What if something more serious happened and Aunt Jewel died? You think it would be right to keep something like that from her?"

"Not only do I think it's right, but I prefer it. If anything ever happens to me please do not tell her. I don't want her anywhere near me, not even my casket."

"If that's how you feel then you're entitled to feel that way," Skye says. "I came out here to tell you the doctor said they are keeping Aunt Jewel overnight to monitor her. Aunt Jewel wants us to go to the house and pick up her make-up, a comb, brush, and a change of clothes."

I laugh, "She's got all of us worried about her and all she's worried about is how she looks."

"She said just because she's sick that doesn't mean she has to look it."

We walk outside and to my surprise Ace is still outside the hospital. "Hold up, Skye. Give me a second." I approach Ace who's looking upward with his hands on his head. "Hey."

"What's up?" He wipes his tears.

"How's your father?" I ask, pretending not to know.

"He didn't make it," he answers.

"I'm really sorry. Are you going to be okay?"

"Yeah, it's surreal. I can't believe this is really happening," he tries to stifle an uncontrollable sob.

Skye interrupts, "Stormey, I have to go. Have him call you or something."

"I'm sorry, she's my ride. Call me if you need to talk." As we leave, I can't help but feel sorry for him. He and his father were so close and now, without warning, he's gone forever.

CHAPTER 10

Ascending Backwards

After being monitored for three days, Aunt Jewel is finally discharged from the hospital. I look at her as we ride home in the back of a cab. It's amazing how similar our features are. Her eyes are my eyes. Her hair is my hair. Our cheekbones are the same. It's like having a fast forward button and being able to see what I'll look like twenty years from now.

She feels me looking at her and turns toward me with a heartwarming smile. "You mother said she was coming over today, so when we arrive home, I'm going to need your help preparing dinner."

"Coming over? For what?"

"I invited her."

"But why? You know we're going to have to keep our eyes on her to make sure she doesn't leave with anything she didn't come with," I complain.

"I'm not worried about that, Stormey," Auntie replies. "I invited Skye over as well. It's been a long time since we all had a chance to have dinner together."

"I don't think this is a good idea, Auntie. I don't want to be in the same room with either of them."

"Stormey, we're family. No matter who does what, how many times we stumble, we will always be here for each other. That's what family does. We forgive each other and we give second, third, and fourth chances. We don't give up on one another. Your DNA won't change and no matter how much you dislike it, everything you are is because of the people you come from."

"Don't remind me. I wish you were my mother. I mean, can you imagine what my life would have been like if I hadn't been born to such a disgraceful woman? Why couldn't my mother have been more like you?"

"Oh, Stormey. I'm honored that you see me the way you do, but you can't keep living your life wishing it were different. You'll never access joy carrying on this way."

"I don't know, Auntie. You always say the past doesn't matter because it's already over, but over isn't undone. I can't help but want to live a pain-free life like others seem to have," I explain.

"Better is a matter of perception," Auntie replies. "You can't always see other people's problems but that doesn't mean they don't exist. The truth is, Stormey, everyone has something they are going through, just came through, or are walking into. *Everyone* goes through something and everyone feels pain but we are all meant to go *through* it, not take residence in it."

She continues, "You can't get stuck and wallow in your circumstances. You must decide whether you want to live your life in pity or in power, as a victim or a victor, making excuses or making things happen. The choice is yours. If you keep moving forward you will see there's a purpose for everything you've been through but you can't get anywhere by ascending backwards."

"Ascending backwards?"

"It's an oxymoron. You can't move forward and backward at the same time. If you continue moving forward while looking in the rearview, you will eventually crash. Whatever you focus on and give your energy and attention to, you will bring into your life. No matter what you perceive it to be, good or bad," she says.

"I know what you're saying, Auntie. I just can't let it go," I say.

"Focus on where you're going, not where you've been, or your coming days will look like the hauntings of yesterday. Decide what kind of life you want, then set your mind on building toward it today."

"I'm focused on not being anything like Amber or Skye."

"I hate to tell you, but with that mindset you're more like them than you think."

"I'm nothing like either of them. Please don't insult me, Auntie."

"It's not meant to be an insult. You have to learn how to shift your perspective to focus on what you wish to have in your life," she says.

"I've been doing the self-talk in the mirror every morning like you taught me."

"It's a good start but there's still more to do. When you learn to control your thoughts, feelings, and responses, then no one will have the authority to make you angry. Your mind is powerful and you must gain control of it. Decide what thoughts are helping you and which ones are hurting and hindering you. You need to learn how to think so you may live the life you desire," she says.

The cab parks in front of our home and Aunt Jewel reaches into her purse to pay the driver's fair. We both exit the cab and walk into the house. "How do I gain control of my thoughts?"

As we enter the house she puts her things away and asks, "Do you know what I do in the mornings when I first wake up?"

"You mean when you are sitting on the floor with your eyes closed and your palms up?"

"Well, that's a part of it. I wake up every morning at four and commune with the Most High. I take a spiritual bath and release all the thoughts and emotions about situations that do not serve my highest good. I visualize what I desire to attract into my life. I pray, journal, and have an intimate conversation with the Most High expressing my gratitude for all the blessings in my life. When you see me I'm usually ending my spiritual practices with meditation.

"I practice being still. Meditation calms your mind. If you sit still long enough you notice your mind is restless, filled with endless chatter. What most people don't know is that we have the ability to cease the noise. Mindfulness is the secret to controlling it. Being aware of your thoughts and how they influence you is how you keep control of your mind instead of letting it control you. The mind is a powerful part of you, but it is not you. If you don't learn how to control it, it can and will take control."

"How do I keep that from happening?" I ask.

"First you need to understand a few things. Your thoughts are prayers. When you think about something often, you give it a substantial amount of energy. Whatever you focus on tends to show up in your life as if it were drawn in by a magnet. What you dwell on influences how you behave. Your actions bring about results of your life, but everything first begins with the thoughts you allow yourself to think."

"Well, that sounds like a good thing."

"It can be, however, it can also be bad, depending on what those thoughts are. If you keep saying you don't want to be like your mother, you'll inevitably become like her in some way because you are giving your mind space to what you don't want instead of what you do want. Focus on the qualities you desire, the life, and the peace that you want. To attract your true desires, shift your focus to what you want. Change your conversation with yourself and watch your life change," she explains further.

"Auntie, I'm really not that deep."

"It's not about being deep, it's about telling yourself a new story. When you sit and dwell on your woes, how do you feel? Do you feel joyful as you think about everything that has brought you great pain? Do you feel like you have a bright future? No, of course not.

"You keep telling yourself this story because although the pain is unpleasant, it is familiar to you and believe it or not, you find comfort in that. This story justifies your need to hold onto the pain, it is the reason you have not been able to move forward. Think about it. Is the story that you are telling yourself even true?"

"Of course it's true! I don't have to make anything up," I respond.

"I'm not asking if the events you fret about really happened. I am asking if the assumptions you've made about the events are true. You are angry with Skye for being with Troy. But why?" she asks.

"She abandoned me! You know that!" I answer.

"Do you think Skye left because she wanted to hurt you? Or do you think she left the situation because she was hurting and Troy offered something better? And what about your mother? You can't even speak her name without going off the deep end. Do you think she became addicted to drugs just to spite you or is it more likely that she gets high to escape her own pain?"

"I have a right to be upset and I don't want to keep listening to you tell me to get over it," I answer.

"I'm not telling you to simply get over it. I'm telling you to stop asking *why me* and simply ask *why*. The choices they made were never about you. They've been thinking of their own suffering and obtaining what they perceive will numb it. It may be selfish, but it surely wasn't an act against you," she says.

"Well, that's the point. They're selfish," I respond.

"And being angry and bitter all the time, how is that working for you? Is that helping you or is it keeping you stuck? When you start to tell yourself the truth about things, you will see that it was never the experience that hurt as much as the way you perceive it. I'm not trying to make light of anything that happened, nor am I condemning you for having strong feelings, but I want you to succeed in life. I want you to go further than you can imagine. Don't you want to leave this town, travel the world and see who you can be?" she asks.

"Of course. That's all I want," I answer.

"What separates the successful from the unsuccessful is re-silience. Successful people have the ability to bounce back from their life's circumstances to reach their goals. I'm trying to help you develop your coping mechanisms. You cannot obtain the promises of today if you are still holding onto the disappointments of yester-day. What was, was. What wasn't, wasn't. What happened, happened. Realize that the past isn't happening in this moment and let it go," she says.

"I don't know how," I admit.

"You must train yourself mentally and emotionally to accept life as it happens, not how you want or think it should be. Until you ac-cept things as they really are, you won't be able to change them," she says.

"What's the point of accepting them if I'm just going to change them anyway?"

"When I say to change things, I am talking about you. You can-not change Amber or Skye. You need to change how you perceive them. Right now you are giving them too much power over the hap-piness of your life. It's time for you to take your power back," she says.

"Will you help me?" I ask.

"Follow me." She directs me into her bedroom.

She sits on the floor and folds her legs, then reaches her hand out and asks me to sit with her. I'm nervous because I'm not sure what this is leading to. I sit down in front of her, face to face.

"Place the palms of your hands on your knees like this," she demonstrates. Still feeling uncomfortable, I do as she says. "Now take a deep breath through your nose like this." I watch her chest rise and her belly fill. "Now breathe out." I watch her chest and belly de-flate. "Now you do it."

I mimic her, all the while wondering how long this will take.

She says, "Okay, let's do it again. Together this time." We inhale and exhale. "Continue to breathe just like that."

It hasn't even been a minute yet and it already feels like an eter-nity.

"You're thinking now, aren't you?" she asks.

"No," I answer.

"Yes, you are, but it's okay," she smiles. "Continue breathing deeply. I want you to monitor the thoughts you are thinking. As you observe them, notice that the thoughts are not you. The thought is just a voice inside of your head. It's like having an internal roommate that's constantly narrating the events of your day from the time you wake 'til the time you sleep."

"But the voice is me," I interrupt.

"Close your eyes," she instructs. I do as she says. "That voice sounds like you, but it's *not you*. If you pay attention, you'll begin to see that you're not the voice because you're the one observing the voice. The voice plays things over and over like a broken record. It keeps you from moving forward because it's still tuned into the past. Through meditation you'll learn how to change the channel. Once you calm your mind, you'll begin to take control and make it work *for you* instead of *against you*."

"Against me how?" I ask.

"If you continue to let that voice run rampant it will eventually drive you crazy. Had that voice been someone else talking to you, you would be ready to fight by now. That's why I taught you affirmations, so you can begin to change how you talk to yourself. You must talk to yourself in a way that makes you feel good about who you are because that's when your life will begin to feel differently.

"If you're constantly telling yourself things that bring you down and make you feel bad, then how do you ever expect to be happy? Whenever you've felt good or bad, there was a thought that occurred first. Therefore, whenever you don't like what you're feeling, you need to check what you're thinking.

"For example, if you make a mistake your first thought is probably something like, "I can't believe I'm so stupid" or "I should've known better." These thoughts automatically make you feel bad about yourself. When you become more aware of your thoughts, you can change your unpleasant thoughts. Do you understand?"

"Yes, I get it," I reply.

"Good. I want you to continue breathing in silence and I will let you know when to open your eyes," she says.

We sit peacefully for five more minutes. It's difficult to control my thoughts, but the deep breathing is making me calmer. When I open my eyes the room seems much brighter.

Aunt Jewel asks, "How do you feel?"

"Sleepy," I reply.

She smiles and says, "That's normal. I sometimes fall asleep afterwards myself. This is something I want us to do together more often. It'll help you break free from the thoughts that keep you shackled to the past and realize you can achieve whatever you dream."

"I also feel peaceful," I add.

"When you breathe deeply it slows your heartrate and causes your blood pressure to lower, which has a calming effect on your body. If you want to live a peaceful life you must first learn how to be at peace."

My phone rings, interrupting my concentration. I look to see who's calling and see it's Ace. I hesitate to answer, but just as it's approaching the last ring I pick up, "Hello?"

"What's going on?" I pause, instantly shifting from calm to anxious, then excited. "Hello?" He says again.

"Yes, I'm here. How...how are you?" I walk to my bedroom and shut the door.

He responds, "I've been better. Did your aunt get out of the hospital?"

"Yes, she actually just got home today," I answer.

"I'm glad she's okay."

"Me too. How are you and your family holding up?"

"Everyone is doing as good as they can, considering."

"And how is Black?" I ask.

"I guess he's alright. I haven't talked to him since we left the hospital," he responds.

"That's surprising, you two seem super close."

"Yeah, we were."

"Did something happen between you two?" I pretend not to know what went down.

"Life happened. I don't really want to talk about it right now."

"I understand. It's a lot to process. Are you still attending your classes?" I try to lighten the conversation.

"Yeah, I can't afford to mess up now that I'm so close to being done," he replies.

"I'm sure your dad would be proud that you haven't lost focus." I instantly regret mentioning his father and there's an awkward pause.

"I gotta take care of something. Can I call you back?" he asks.

"Uh...yeah, no problem," I facepalm myself for mentioning his dad again. After hanging up, I head to the kitchen where Aunt Jewel is preparing dinner.

"Was that Ace? Where has he been? Y'all planning another date?" she inquires.

"I'm not sure if he'll feel up to it any time soon. His dad passed away while you were in the hospital."

"Oh, the poor guy. How is he handling it?" she asks.

"I don't know. They were close but he seems to be handling it well, I guess."

"I have to pray for him and his family to get through this difficult transition." Aunt Jewels adds the chopped vegetables to the pot.

"I thought you said Amber and Skye were coming over for dinner," I state.

"Skye called and said she can't make it. We'll see about your mom but I wouldn't count on it because Skye was supposed to be her ride. It was a nice thought that we would all be together, but life happens," she says.

"Well, I'm not mad about it. Do you need any help with dinner?" I ask.

"I'll be fine. Besides, you look really tired. Go ahead and lay down," she insists.

"You're right, I'm exhausted." I lay down on my bed and fall asleep instantly.

CHAPTER 11

Casualty of Luxury

Startled by the light tapping on my bedroom window, I open my eyes and look at the clock. It's four twenty-two in the morning. The tapping persists. I rub the sleep out of my eyes and peep through the curtain.

"Come down and open the door!" Skye harshly whispers.

I hurry to open the door. Looking at her disheveled hair, ripped dress, and swollen face, I say, "You look a mess! What happened?"

She brushes past me and walks straight to my bedroom. I lock the front door and follow behind her. She sits on the bed. "What are you doing here so late and why didn't you just call my phone?" I ask.

Skye rocks from side to side and begins to sob. I wrap my arms around her. Whatever happened, I'm sure Troy was behind it. Skye looks up at me with puffy eyes and mascara running down her face. "I'm tired. I just want to lay down," she says with a swollen lip.

"Let me get a washcloth to clean you up." I return to the room and wipe her face softly, patiently waiting for her to say something.

"Where are you coming from?" I ask.

"Troy and I went out to celebrate Tyrone's birthday," she says.

"Who's Tyrone?"

"Troy's best friend," she answers.

"Oh," I utter.

She continues, "I wanted to dance, but Troy didn't, so I danced with Tyrone."

"Why would you do that?"

"He offered when Troy refused," she explains.

"You know how Troy is. Didn't you think he'd get jealous?"

"I made sure he was okay with it first. He knows how much I love to dance and said it was cool."

"And you believed him?"

"Tyrone and I danced for maybe, three songs, before heading back to the VIP with everyone else."

"That was a long time considering Troy can't allow you out of his sight for three seconds."

"When we got back, Troy was upset but I thought it was because of something that happened while I was away," she continues. "He poured himself another drink and I suggested he slow down since he was driving. He yelled at me, saying I was trying to tell him what to do. That's when I knew he was too drunk to reason with so I went to the restroom."

"What happened to your face though?" I urge impatiently.

"When I walked out the restroom a guy grabbed my arm and said, "You just going to walk past me like that?" I turned around and it was Black."

"Black? Ace's Black?" I ask.

"Yeah, he was smiling at me. I looked to see if Troy was watching but he wasn't. Black noticed that I was nervous so he asked if I was there with someone. I told him I was and that I had to get back so he said to call him when I broke away.

"When I made it back to VIP, Troy was pouring another drink so I asked if something was wrong. He didn't say anything so I said, "This just isn't your norm. That's all." Troy picked up his shot glass and drank it down. Then without even looking at me he asked who the dude was that grabbed my arm. I tried to play dumb but that made him angrier. Finally, I just told him I didn't know who Black was, but that he tried to talk to me but I said I was already taken.

"When everyone started getting ready to leave I asked Troy if he was ready and without saying a word, he just got up and we started walking out. Then he started trippin' again talking about I was extra friendly and that's when Black walked past, and I looked away, but not fast enough. I started to go get the car but Troy snatched my hair. Then he punched me in the face so hard that I hit the ground.

"He was yelling, asking if I thought he was a fool and saying I wasn't loyal because I wanted to get everyone's attention. Said I was embarrassing him in front of his boys.

"I quickly stood up, hoping not too many people noticed what happened. He wasn't done though. He said I was messing around with another dude in his face. He tried to hit me again but Black grabbed him. I ran away but he followed me and snatched the keys. Told me to go home with that dread head, talking about Black, since I was for the streets.

"That's when Tyrone grabbed him and said that was enough. Troy stared at me for a few seconds and left with Tyrone. Black gave me a ride here."

Tears well up in my eyes as rage heats my blood. I look at her, observing her swollen face. "Do you think he knows you're here?"

Skye responds, "He knows I don't have anywhere else to go."

I ask, "But do you think he'll come here tonight?"

She shakes her head. "He's too drunk to do anything."

"You need to get into the shower and clean yourself up. I'll get you something to sleep in. The last thing you want is for Auntie to see you like this."

Skye nods her head. "She'd flip out. I'll leave before she wakes up. I don't want to upset her."

"Leave and go where?" I ask.

"You don't have to worry, I'll be okay, Stormey."

"Nothing about you is okay right now."

Skye walks away without saying anything and goes into the bathroom. I put on a pot of water to make some Chamomile tea to help her relax. She comes out looking much better.

"Get dressed while I get you some ice."

"Thank you," she says softly.

I walk back in the bedroom with our tea, sit on the bed next to Skye, and say, "You know you can stay here in the spare bedroom. It'll be just like old times."

"I just don't know what came over him tonight," Skye says.

"You sound like you're considering his feelings," I reply.

"What do you mean?"

"Aren't you going to move out?" I demand. "I know you aren't thinking about going back to him after this?"

"I don't know. He's never done anything like this before. He had way too much to drink tonight," Skye responds.

"I can't believe this. He put his hands on you. He's an asshole!" I snap.

"Stormey, you don't understand. It's not that simple," Skye responds. "He's a good guy and he takes care of me. I can't have it all."

There is a moment of silence between us because I can't believe what I'm hearing. "It's obvious you're not in love with him. He doesn't do the things you like and he doesn't make you feel good either, but he gives you money and buys you nice gifts. I know you think I'm silly for wanting to be with a guy that makes me feel good, but isn't that what it's all about? What's the point of being in a relationship with someone that says they love you, but leaves you bloody on the sidewalk?"

"Stormey, you don't get it. I don't care about feelings. I care about where I sleep, what I eat, what's on my back, and the places I can go. I know my time is limited and I'm not going to waste it with some broke dude that makes me feel warm and fuzzy. When I get old enough to tell my story, I want to have a story to tell. I'm going places and doing things with Troy that I wouldn't be able to do without him."

"What are you thinking? Are you even thinking at all? This is not you, Skye. You deserve better than this. I mean, you are better than this."

She rolls her eyes and says, "You're too naive to understand."

"I know that you are in love with the lifestyle that comes with being with a guy like Troy, but what about happiness? Are you happy, Skye?" I pick up my handheld mirror and hold it to her face, forcing her to look at her reflection. "Look in the mirror, Skye. Look at what's happening to you. Is it worth it? Is this the price you're willing to pay? Are you prepared to be a casualty of luxury?"

"I'm tired, Stormey. I'm going to bed." Skye moves the mirror out of her face and lays down.

I don't know why I keep allowing myself to get dragged into her drama. It's clear that we're never going to agree. "Don't go back there," I plead. "Promise that you won't go back there. Okay? Can you promise me that?"

She's quiet and her eyes are closed. I don't know if she's asleep or just ignoring me. I climb into bed and lay down beside her. "Goodnight."

CHAPTER 12

Lost on Purpose

I'm relieved when I wake up and see Skye is still asleep. I hope she never goes back to Troy but knowing her, she probably will.

I start my morning routine in hopes of finishing before she wakes so I don't have to endure her excessive teasing. She thinks the things I've learned from Aunt Jewel are silly but Aunt Jewel taught us the importance of starting our days off by connecting to our spirit and focusing on our higher calling. Skye doesn't appreciate the value in slowing down, but sometimes you have to slow down in order to speed things up.

Being alive and healthy is a blessing, especially considering my origin story. Aunt Jewel taught me about God when I was young. She said I was protected and that my life had purpose. I believe her. If I didn't, I don't think I would've survived this chaotic world or even made it this far.

I close my eyes to visualize my desires coming to pass. I'm filled with gratitude while envisioning my artwork being admired and purchased by people all over the world but I find it hard to concentrate this morning. My attention continuously drifts to thoughts about Ace.

Initially, I wasn't interested in being in a relationship with him but he treats me the way Aunt Jewel said a man should and I'm happy I gave him a chance. Skye's phone rings and interrupts my concentration.

"Hello?" She answers. "What do you mean?" Skye walks out the room so I won't hear her conversation but I know she's talking to Troy.

When she comes back and sees that I'm stretching she says, "I see Auntie has you on some BS. What is that? Yoga?"

"Good morning to you, too." I continue stretching.

"Good morning."

"What did Troy want?"

"Who said it was Troy?"

"What did he say?" I persist.

"Did you know Aunt Jewel is cooking breakfast?" She says evasively.

"Yeah, I smell the turkey bacon."

"Well, come on before she thinks we are being rude by staying in the bedroom this late," Skye jokes. She motions for me to get in front of her as she follows me into the kitchen. Aunt Jewel already has the table set for three.

Skye asks, "Were you expecting company?"

Aunt Jewel replies, "No, I heard you come in this morning. Breakfast is almost done. Go ahead and take your seats."

We both sit down but neither of us are willing to say the first word. We remain in an awkward silence while Aunt Jewel serves our breakfast. We all hold hands as she blesses the food. While eating in silence for several minutes, I see Aunt Jewel out the corner of my eye looking as if she is reading our minds. I feel uncomfortable and can tell Skye does too.

I break the tension and ask, "How did you sleep last night, Auntie?"

She replies, "I slept well until I heard you two talking this morning. I was too tired to get up, though."

"Oh."

Skye looks up from her plate. "Sorry for coming in so late. I was on this side of town and was too tired to make it all the way home. I didn't mean to disturb you."

Aunt Jewel smiles, "There's no reason to be sorry. My home will always be open to you girls no matter what the hour is. You'll always have a safe haven here."

"Thanks for understanding, Auntie," Skye says.

"From the looks of you, you were more than tired last night. If I didn't know any better, I'd think that you were in a fight. You always have bruised easily."

Skye, noticeably uncomfortable, comes clean. "Troy and I got into a fight last night. He was drinking more than usual and behaved in a way I've never seen before. I don't know what came over him."

"Well, that's why they call it liquid courage. It fueled him to do what was already inside. It's up to you to see him for who he truly is or to continue believing that he'll someday turn into the man you hope he'll be."

Skye responds, "But he's good to me, Auntie. He takes care of me and treats me better than anyone else ever has. I don't know what was going on with him, but Troy *is* a good guy."

I'm flabbergasted to see Skye jump to Troy's defense so easily.

Auntie quickly replies, "What's so good about the way your face looks right now? What's so good about not being able to be who you are and playing small because you fear bruising his ego? What's good about being afraid to go home at night? You tell me Skye, what's so good about that?"

Skye's agitation shows as she responds, "I thought you'd understand, but you don't get it."

Aunt Jewel asks, "What is it that I don't get, Skye? Help me understand. You're too beautiful and too precious to be anyone's punching bag. There's nothing in this world that you can do that's bad enough to make it okay for anyone to put their hands on you, ever."

Aunt Jewel's understandably upset. Skye is too, for that matter.

"He called me this morning to tell me he's sorry and he loves me. He promised that it'll never happen again and I believe him. It never happened before and it wouldn't have happened last night if he wasn't drinking so much. Besides, he said he bought me something really nice." Skye stares off into the distance. "I can't wait to see what he got me."

Aunt Jewel grabs Skye's hands. "Look at me, Skye. You don't know love," she begins.

"I do know what love is!" Skye quickly snaps back.

"You think you do, but you have no idea. Unfortunately, you've grown to believe that love is expressed through pain, tears, abuse, cheating, beating, breaking up to make up, or that it can be bought. That is not love. This boy does not love you. He loves to control you but he does not love you," Aunt Jewel responds.

"Troy does not control me! He takes care of me. This one incident does not define our entire relationship. He said he's sorry and I believe him."

"Any man that can raise his hands to your face does not love you. Love is God's purest expression and can never be tainted this way. It doesn't matter what that boy buys you, it'll never fill the void within you that makes you think that you are not enough. You don't need expensive things to give your life value. That void is like a bottomless pit and no matter how many things you throw in it, it will never be full until you fill it with the right thing."

"Let me guess," Skye barks, "that right thing is God. Spare me. Where was God when I was sleeping on the floor with hunger pangs? Where was God when my mother was trying to pimp me out to the landlord to pay the rent? You can say what you want about Troy, but he took care of me when God wouldn't, and his love is the only love I know!"

"What he's giving you isn't love. You're being distracted with shiny objects that block you from seeing that behind all of the smoke and mirrors nothing is really there," says Aunt Jewel.

"Believe what you want, but I know the truth about Troy and I know that what we have is real. I have to get ready before he gets here to pick me up. Can I be excused?" Skye asks.

"You're running away from what you had no control over as a little girl but you're running in the wrong direction. If you keep running you'll remain a lost little girl, unable to find her way home. Material possessions and a few fun thrills are not worth your soul," Aunt Jewel raises her voice.

There's a loud knock at the door and I instantly feel fire shoot through my veins. I already know it's Troy without having to get out my seat. Skye gets up from the table but I don't bother to move. I stare in disbelief while watching her prance to the door.

I used to look up to Skye but she is no longer the same. The things she says are so irrational that if I didn't know better, I'd think Troy had gotten her hooked on drugs. I don't know what Troy did to her, but I want my sister back. I look over at Aunt Jewel as she stares at Skye. She walks ever so slowly toward the door. I can hear Skye screaming, sounding extremely excited about something. I jump out of my seat and run to the door to see what's going on.

I'm in disbelief. She's making out with Troy right in front of the house and seems super happy. Aunt Jewel hesitantly walks down the stairs but I'm frozen in astonishment.

Skye looks at me and asks, "Aren't you coming down to look too, Stormey?"

Skye pulls Aunt Jewel toward the brand new white Maserati Ghibli parked in the driveway. She opens the doors and exposes the black interior with red leather seats. The rims are shiny and the tires look wet. Troy looks proud. He walks over to Skye and asks, "Don't you want to take it for a ride?"

She shrills ecstatically, "Yes, let's go!" She gives Aunt Jewel a hug and whispers, "I told you he loves me."

I run off the porch and grab Skye's shoulders, hoping to help her get her sense back. "What are you doing? Are you really this chick now? You can be bought?"

"Stormey, get off me!" She yells.

I yell back, not caring if Troy hears every word. "No! We used to stay up at night and vow that we'd never get caught up in the lifestyle of fast money and material possessions, of women staying with men that are no good and who treat them poorly just because they buy them pretty things. Now this man has beat you and all it takes is a pretty car to make you forget the bruises on your body?"

As she pulls away from me, Skye demands, "You know nothing about life. You know nothing about love. Stay here in your small world with your modest possessions while I live a life that you can't even afford to dream about."

I watch her get into the driver's seat of the car. I'm fuming with anger and disbelief. Troy gets into the passenger seat with a smile on his face. He sends a nasty wink my way, assuring me that he's in charge. Skye waves excitedly and blows the horn as she races down the street.

I glare at the white Maserati as it moves further and further away. I remain unmoved until I can no longer see the car. Until I can no longer feel. I'm numb.

Aunt Jewel looks at me as she holds the door to the house. "Come back inside." Once inside, she stands there for a few seconds before speaking. "Remember what I told you? This is one of those moments. You can't live her life for her. When she gets tired, she'll change. Until then, there's nothing you can do. You just need to be ready to hold her when she needs you. And she *will* need you."

"You're right, Auntie. I think it's time for me to give up on her."

She responds, "I'm not suggesting that you give up on your sister. I'm telling you not to lose focus of your own life by being consumed with what she's doing with hers."

Today it's been made clear that Skye is a lost cause, just like my mother.

CHAPTER 13

Tasting Candy

"Thanks for chilling with me today. It means a lot that we can hang out like homies as well," Ace states.

"You don't have to thank me. I enjoy spending time with you and I like being able to see you in your element," I explain.

"Well, come inside with me, I gotta see Tone real quick," Ace pulls into the carwash parking lot. We get out the car and I follow him inside.

"What's up, Ace?" Greets Tone.

"What's good, Unc?" Ace fist bumps him. "Stormey, this is my uncle Tone."

"I finally get to meet you. Ace talks about you so much that I feel like I already know you. You're even more beautiful than I imagined."

"Thank you, Ace speaks highly of you also."

Tone turns his attention back to Ace. "What are you doing here today?"

"I gotta check last night's paperwork to make sure all the numbers from last night's shift are consistent with this morning's deposit."

"You're always on point. It's good to know that I can leave everything in your hands without worry. That's a special character trait that not everyone has."

"I'm working for the position I want, not the one I have."

"You'll get there sooner than you think. Keep it up."

"And when's that exactly?"

"Patience grasshopper. Patience," Tone replies.

After doing his morning check, Ace shouts, "Unc, I'm going to open the doors, but I gotta run to the bank to drop off last night's deposit."

"Who was supposed to do the drop last night?" Tone asks. "Y'all know how I feel about having large amounts of money in here especially when we open in the morning. If someone catches word that we're leaving money around they'll try and hit us like they been doing the other spots around here."

"Don't worry, Unc, I'll talk to the night manager. We'll get it squared away." Ace opens the gates and doors to the wash.

I point to a car pulling up. I recognize the eggplant Mercedes. "I thought you said no one gets their car washed this early."

Rich rolls in and greets him, "What's good, Lil' King? How you and your mom holding up?"

"We're hanging in there."

Rich nods. "I lost my Pops when I was young and I know it isn't easy. Kind of leaves a hole in your soul that nothing else can fill. Now with your pops gone you gotta be the man and I know waxing down cars isn't bringing in no dough. I could see if you owned the place, but how much is Tone really paying you? Stop wasting your time here. Come out of this worker bee mode and get some real money. Your father's name still carries some weight out here, but it won't for long. You better use your old man's clout to your advantage while people are still willing to look out for you."

"I heard all this talk before, Rich. You still haven't said anything to get my attention," Ace responds.

"Working these crazy hours wiping down cars ain't never going to be enough. What's the end game here?"

I can see Ace pondering Rich's words. "My handiwork and dedication will pay off. I know it."

"When you have an opportunity of a lifetime, you have to seize it. Time waits for no one." As if he can feel Ace warming up to the idea, Rich continues, "Look, I'll tell you what. Here's my number. When you get off work hit me up. I have something you want."

"And what would that be?" Ace asks.

"I have information about your father." Rich gives Ace his number.

"What about my father? Are you saying you know who killed him?"

"Call me and I'll tell you where to meet me. We can't talk here."

Ace, appearing to be deep in thought, reluctantly says, "Okay. Are you getting a wash?"

"Why else would I be here?" Before he gets into his car, he says, "Make sure you wax it too."

As Rich pulls off, he stops to say, "I expect to hear from you."

Ace replies, "Bet."

Tone comes out of the office. "What was Rich talking about?"

"The same ol' same ol'. You know how it goes." Ace shrugs his shoulders.

"I don't like him," I add. "Why couldn't he tell you what he had to say while he was here?"

Tone says, "Believe me, that isn't a phone call you want to make. Besides I'm grooming you to be a businessman."

Ace responds, "And exactly when are you planning on showing me the part about how to actually run a business? Right now you got me running ragged up in here washing cars and sweating like a slave."

Tone says, "That's what's wrong with you young dudes today. Everyone wants immediate gratification and no one wants to work for the results. I'm giving you something valuable but you can't even see it. The grunt work you're doing now builds character. You want to be successful? Well, having strong character is how you stay successful. Once you understand that, I can begin to teach you the ins and outs of entrepreneurship. Besides, we are expanding and over the next few months we are opening three more locations. I need you to help me maintain it as my partner."

"You're finally about to make me a partner?"

Tone says, "Listen, you may think you need to get out there and make moves, but I've lived that life before, and there is nothing out there but destruction. Being legit is the only way."

"Unc, you work hard for what you got, but what you make in a year, they make in a few minutes. Don't you ever miss getting it like that?"

"Let me tell you something. I was given something that not too many people walk away with, a second chance. I was out in the streets. I had money, cars, clothes, women, and respect. I was living life at the top of the food chain. My crew was tight. We operated under the code, *no one talks, everyone walks*. I made the mistake of letting young guys in on the game. It only took one of them to forget the code. Next thing you know, the feds were busting in my door at four in the morning. They walked me out of my home practically naked. After everything was said and done, I was facing up to twenty-five years. You hear me? I was making good money but once I calculated that time, the math no longer added up."

"Damn, Unc, that's almost longer than I've been living."

"Sabrina was pregnant with Lil' Tone at the time. She was a good woman and swore she'd wait for me. I knew she believed that, but I also knew another man was about to raise my son. I was gonna miss out on his first smile, his first step, first day of school, graduation, twenty-five birthdays and Christmases. I would miss every moment that brought him into manhood.

"I got to thinking about what I was doing. The men your father and I entered the game with were all getting locked up, one by one. The ones that didn't make it to jail were killed. I was done chasing mirages. I dropped to my knees and prayed for a miracle."

"Apparently God heard your prayers because you're here to tell the story."

"Yes, He heard me. I told Him I would change my life around and I kept my word. I took heed to my warning the first time because I knew it wasn't guaranteed that I would live to see another one. I didn't have any work experience so I went into business for myself. In reality, I was already an entrepreneur. If I could successfully sell drugs, then I could do anything. I just needed to bankrupt one business and start a new one. Now I sleep peacefully at night."

Ace says, "That's heavy. I couldn't imagine losing that much time. You wouldn't be making any money at all locked up."

Tone looks at Ace. "I don't care about the money, I care about the memories I would've lost. Money comes and goes but it doesn't compare to the memories that a life well lived can bring."

"I hear you, Unc. I'm about to run this deposit to the bank."

I follow behind Ace and say, "It was nice meeting you, Uncle Tone."

Ace glances at his phone. "Sorry, Stormey. That took longer than I planned."

"You weren't really listening to what Uncle Tone was talking about, were you?"

"Let me ask you something," he replies. "If your aunt was killed and someone had some information about her, would you forget it or would you try to find out what they know?" Ace turns around and looks back at the wash. "I think about all the time and sweat I've put into working, hoping one day to get a big payday. I've washed and waxed so many cars I've lost count. Today I got the news I've hoped for, twice. I'm finally seeing the fruits of my labor and I may finally get answers about my father's death. So, to answer your question, yes, I'm making that phone call."

"I understand you wanting answers and all, but I can see what kind of person Rich is and I won't date someone who's mixed up in the streets. That would be the end of you and me," I cross my arms over my chest.

Ace looks deep in thought but doesn't respond.

CHAPTER 14

Thoughtless Thinking, Sightless Seeing

"Hello?" Ace answers his phone. "Just text me the address and I'll be on my way."

"Who was that?" I ask.

"Rich. I know you made your thoughts about him clear already so if you want me to drop you off first, then I will, but I have to go see what he has for me."

"Is it safe for me to go with you?" I ask.

"I wouldn't do anything to put you in harm's way."

"I'll go with you as long as you are sure there's no funny business going on."

"I promise." Ace proceeds to drive into a warehouse parking lot.

"What exactly does Rich do here?" We exit the car and walk towards the door.

"Stormey, just go with the flow. We're just going to talk. Stop looking worried."

I attempt to look unbothered as we arrive at the door where a large, muscular male is standing inside of the doorway. He immediately pats Ace down, checking for weapons. He does the same to me and I feel even more uneasy. After finding nothing on us, he says, "He's with someone. Wait here."

"Ace, this is a bit much, I don't feel comfortable. Maybe I shouldn't have come."

"Stormey, I promise there is nothing to worry about. This is just protocol for someone like him. I wouldn't put you in harm's way, I really just came because he said he had some important information for me." Ace looks down at his watch impatiently. "I told this dude I have another appointment. I wish he'd hurry the hell up."

After what feels like an eternity, the guard returns. "He'll see you now."

Another door opens and he signals for a different guard to escort Ace and me to the back. As we walk through, there are several guys standing around with faces hard as stone. I can't help but feel unwelcomed.

"Sit right here." Ace leads me to a couch just outside of Rich's office.

Rich opens the door and says, "Lil' King!" Then he looks at me and says, "I see she's still hanging in there."

"Yeah, we're doing alright," Ace replies.

"Come in and have a seat." I see Rich sit in front of a chess board.

"Isn't this a two-player game?" Ace follows him into the office. The guard closes the door and stands outside of it next to me. I can faintly hear what they are saying.

"I like to play by myself to consider the board from all angles. It keeps me sharp. You play?" Rich asks.

"Nah, I never could get into it. Chess is a game for nerds," Ace answers.

"You should learn to play because chess is a game of war. If you want longevity then you have to be able to see the next move and beyond," Rich explains. "Sit down, let me show you something. The objective of this game is to get the other player's king. That's this piece all the way back here. The king is weak on his own and is only as strong as his army, which are these other pieces you see surrounding it."

"How do you get to the king?"

"You have to infiltrate his army."

"How do you do that?"

"You have to know the function of each piece before you start to move." Rich picks up the game piece next to the king. "This is the queen, the coldest piece on the board. The king can move in whichever direction he wants, but he only moves one space at a time. The queen, on the other hand, can move however she wants. She is the enforcer and gets things done by luring other pieces into her trap and taking them out. The king is safe as long as his queen is around."

"What's up with these. What they do?" Ace points to other pieces on the board.

"The rook moves front to back or left to right and the bishop moves diagonally only. They are more significant than the pawns, but not much. This one in between them is the knight. The knight is the most unique because it can jump over other pieces to make its move.

"This whole front line is comprised of pawns. You have to be leery of these pieces right here. People are quick to underestimate a pawn because they are the weakest and get eliminated quick. If a pawn is smooth enough to move through the opponent's army and end up on the other side of the board then you will be looking at a pawn making power moves like a queen."

"I got my girl sitting out there waiting on me," Ace states impatiently.

"Pay attention, it's right in your face," Rich responds.

"No disrespect, but can we make this fast because I have somewhere else to be."

"Let's cut to the chase. Your father was the king. Someone infiltrated his army and eliminated him. Have you ever asked yourself, how was that possible when his entire army remains standing?"

"What are you trying to say? You think it was an inside job?" Ace asks angrily.

"What I'm saying is that your father ran the coldest operation in the streets for a long time. He owned half the city and had the best product out there. Everybody wanted what he had but was afraid to make a move on him. It's obvious that he slipped up and trusted someone he shouldn't have. Once the pawn got inside, it started making power moves like a queen. Now your father is no longer here but his product is still moving. Why should someone else reap all the benefits when you are the legitimate heir? Here, take this."

"What is it?"

"Consider it a gift. You will find the answers you're looking for inside that envelope."

"Nah, I can't take it, I told you I'm not into that." Ace puts it back on the desk.

"It's not what you think it is. Open it up. Trust me," Rich insists.

I hear the paper ripping through the door as Ace opens the envelope. "Whose burner phone is this?" Ace asks.

"Turn it on and look at the messages."

"There are text messages here from the night my father was killed. Someone texted this phone saying to get in position and strike as soon as he leaves the diner. Whose phone is this and how did you get it?" Ace asks rapidly in confusion.

"Let's just say while taking out my own trash, a rat gave me information that would benefit you. Like I said, it's a gift. You should know the snakes around you."

"Who sent these messages?"

"I can't give you all the answers. Some things you have to figure out for yourself but that phone is a major key to the puzzle. Who has the most to gain? Study the board. How are the pieces still moving? The game should be over if you don't have a king, right? You're in a unique position Lil' King. You can make moves like no one else in the game. Out of respect for your father they will let you in and because everyone thinks you're harmless, they will underestimate you, just like the pawn. That's your leverage. Not only can you make it all the way in and start making power moves, but you also get to see who had the most to gain since your father's elimination," Rich states.

"Who was that?"

"That's what only you can find out, but you can't go knocking on doors and asking questions. You gotta be inside to get inside information. Remember, this is the game of chess. Be ready to make your next move."

"This sounds like a game that I don't want to play. If you know who it is just tell me."

"You and your family deserve to know the truth but you'll have to find it on your own."

Ace hesitates, "This is crazy."

"They killed your father, no matter how clean you want to keep your nose, you can't let this ride. Knowing that you had the opportunity to get the answers but didn't will definitely burn in your soul and eat away at you. You can't sleep with that," Rich replies.

There's a pause. Ace hesitantly says, "Bet. Good looking out."

"Fa' sho'," responds Rich.

Ace comes out of the office. I look for the phone I heard them talking about, but don't see it.

"Let's go," Ace grabs my hand. He leads me out of the warehouse as I nervously watch over my shoulders to check the surroundings. As he drives off, I reflect on what I just heard. It was disturbing and I want to ask how he feels, but I don't want him to know I was eavesdropping.

"What did he want to talk to you about?" I ask.

"He wanted to tell me something about my dad." Ace appears lost in thought.

"Like what?"

"My dad used to say, "The love you find in the streets, like candy, is artificially sweet. Don't get caught up in the daydream. Keep a watchful eye on the ones around you because someone is always watching to catch you slipping and take what you got." He said that so many times, and his words never rung truer."

"What are you saying, Ace?" I ask with worry.

"I don't know. For some reason, after talking to Rich, I feel like I'm closer to knowing the truth," Ace answers.

"The truth about what?"

"King's death," Ace responds. We pull up to the carwash where Tone is standing outside. Ace rolls the window down.

"Ace Boogie! What's going on? You're late!" Tone greets.

"Yeah, my bad, Unc. I had a meeting that ran long. I meant to call, but it's just a lot going on," Ace replies.

"You know these dudes don't do anything right. Everything was out of order when I got in here." Tone adds, "Hi, Stormey."

I nod.

"It's good to know I'm missed. It seems this place can't run without me," Ace laughs.

"Just make sure to be here so we don't have to find out," says Tone. "Where's the case of cleaner so we can get back rolling in here?"

"It's in the trunk. I'll get it." Ace steps out of the car.

"You don't have to get out. I'll grab it," replies Tone.

"Well, I don't want to see you throw your back out, old man," Ace jokes. He steps out of the car and the black flip phone falls to the ground.

"When did you get a flip phone? I haven't had one of those in ages. I didn't even know they still made them." Tone's eyes light up.

"I got it from Rich a few minutes ago." Ace opens the trunk and I find myself eavesdropping once again as a I sit in the front seat quietly.

"Rich? Since when did you start dealing with him?" Tone asks with his brows furrowed.

"He thinks my father's death was an inside job and he gave me this burner phone. Said it belongs to the person that killed my dad. From the way he was talking I could tell the owner of it is dead but whoever sent these messages is still alive."

"He just gave it to you? No strings attached? You know you can't trust him."

"There are text messages on here from the night my father was killed." Ace hands Tone the phone.

"This feels like a set up. What are you going to do about it, get yourself killed too?"

"No, I want revenge. All I have to do is find out who this phone belongs to."

"How do you expect to do that? And how did Rich get this phone anyway? The person that did this has the heart of a killer; you do not. Your heart isn't hard enough. Let the police do their job. Finish your last semester of school so you can get your degree and put this vigilante mess behind you."

"I need answers!" Ace's breath becomes labored and his chest rises and falls rapidly. "The fact that the person that had my father killed is reaping the benefits with no repercussions is something I can't accept. I thought if anybody would understand, it would be you." The corners of his mouth are now turned downward and his jaws are tense.

"What I understand is that you're a young man that has reached a crossroad. My life, yours, and everyone else's is a culmination of choices. You have a choice to make and whatever you decide will alter your life path in a major way. Not to sound harsh, but your father made his choice and he died as result of it. Don't be a fool and do the same," Tone states defiantly.

"Don't let Rich trick you into becoming a part of the vicious cycle that is destroying our community from the inside out. You are supposed to be different. You're supposed to make it out because your father and I both did all we could to break you free from the shackles that come from growing up here."

"How can I live with myself knowing I did nothing when given the opportunity?" Ace responds.

"Following behind Rich won't make it right. Use your head. Rich is a flightless bird that has never been anywhere, nor done anything. This hood and the game are all he knows. You're in school to legitimately expose yourself to people that are living the way you dream. What can a lost man show you other than how to be lost too? Get your thoughts together because once you get in the streets you may never find your way out."

"You got out," Ace points out.

"I am the exception to the rule. Don't make dumb choices expecting to be lucky. You can't do what everyone else has done and expect things to turn out differently for you. Doing something new is the only way out," Tone replies.

"I hear you, Unc," Ace says.

"You're grown now and your life is only yours to live. If getting involved with guys like Rich is what you're choosing, then there is no need for you to come back here. I don't need this type of karma in my place of business. You have some thinking to do but you can't do it here," Tone says.

I respect Uncle Tone's stance.

"Damn, it's like that?"

"Rich is not just helping you out of the goodness of his heart. Don't let your desperation to know the truth blind you from seeing the bigger picture. I love you as if you were my own, but I cannot, and I will not, have this type of foolishness around me. I will not risk all that I built, not even for you. You need to think carefully about your next move. If you come back, I will know what you chose. If not, then I too, will know what you chose. I can't afford to put my life at risk because you haven't found the value in your own," says Tone.

Ace closes his eyes while breathing hard, shallow breaths. "My father risked his life every day to make sure I was okay. It's my duty to make sure that the person that killed him is dealt with justly."

"You can be whomever you desire to be, but you will never be great if you can't see yourself that way. If you only see yourself as the dopeman's son, then that is all you'll ever be."

With tears welling up in his eyes, Ace raises his voice and declares, "My family's life is changed forever because of this coward and I'm going to find out who it is."

I'm shocked, I can't believe Ace is even entertaining something so risky. He's so blinded by his grief that he doesn't realize he's making a mistake that could cost him his life.

CHAPTER 15

Mending Hearts

The house phone rings. I pick up the receiver and learn Aunt Jewel beat me to it. Just as I'm hanging up I hear my mother's voice and roll my eyes. She never calls unless she needs something and whatever it is, I don't care. I hang up and walk back to my room to finish straightening up.

"Stormey, I need you to come with me." Aunt Jewel stands in my bedroom doorway.

"Go with you where, Auntie?" I ask.

"I need to run an errand but I don't want to ride by myself. Come on girl."

"What kind of errand?" Knowing she just hung up with my mother has me feeling uneasy. I don't want to do anything that has to do with her.

"Are you going to ask twenty questions or are you going to get ready? I'll be outside warming up the car. Hurry up." Aunt Jewel walks away without answering me.

I put my coat on and walk outside to get in the car. It's still freezing. As we pull out the driveway I notice she appears anxious. I'm not sure what's going on, but I know it has to do with Amber. After a while we pull into the parking lot of a brick building.

"Come inside with me."

"What is this place?" I ask, although the sign clearly reads Police Precinct. The scent of foul musk and liquor hits my nostrils as we walk inside. Judging by the unkempt man sleeping in the chair, I assume it doubles as a safe haven for the local vagabonds passing through. The peeling paint, the badly stained linoleum floors that look as if they've never been mopped or polished, contribute to my feeling of disease.

"Do you know why we're here, Stormey?" Aunt Jewel asks.

"That's what I'm trying to figure out," I answer.

"It's been a long time since I've been in here. Every time I walk through these doors, I silently petition with my heart that it'll be the last." She walks up to the desk where a woman in uniform stares at her as if she's spreading the plague with her presence. This woman is obviously not in a pleasant mood and the way she's slouched over the counter using her phone shows she isn't interested in doing her job either.

"Good evening, Ma'am, I am here to post a bond. Do you have an Amber Knights in your custody?"

"Ugh! I knew it! I can't believe you brought me here for this!" I cry out.

"Let me see," the officer says without even looking at her roster. "Yeah, Amber's here. She's always here. That'll be five hundred and sixty-seven dollars. You need to have the exact amount because we do not give change." Without looking up from her phone she points to the sign behind her head and continues, "No checks. No credit cards. Do you have the money now?"

Aunt Jewel places her purse on the counter. "Yes, I have it now. I've been here enough to know that I need to have singles on hand." She reaches inside, pulls out her wallet, counts her money, and hands it to the officer who finally looks up. She walks away for a few moments before coming back with paperwork for Aunt Jewel to sign.

She hands Aunt Jewel her copy and says, "Have a seat. It'll be a few minutes before she comes out." Aunt Jewel starts to sit but decides against it. I don't blame her since this place looks infested.

"See what you have to look forward to?" Aunt Jewel asks me.

"No, I don't. She knows better than to call me. I'd never show up for her," I respond.

"That may be so, but she's not who I'm talking about. What are you going to do when you receive a similar call from your sister?"

"What? Why would Skye call me from jail?"

"She's living fast and loose with Troy. I've tried not to judge her, hoping she'd come around. Now that I see what he's capable of and the fact that she turns a blind eye to it, it makes me wonder what else she's pretending not to know. Your mother told me he's dealing drugs. I had my suspicions, but now I know. It seems like everyone wants to live as the exception and ignore the rules. We can look at those around us and see what not to and what to do simply by paying attention. We all think we're different when the truth is we're all the same because the universal laws of nature apply to us all equally," she explains.

"Well, Skye isn't an addict nor prostitute, so I don't see it happening," I say.

"Don't be narrow minded," she says. "There have been so many nights I've been awoken from my sleep and secretly wanted to leave her here but I've never had what it takes to leave my sister behind."

The doors open and she stops talking. I look up to see Amber walking towards us. Her hair is scattered all over her head and standing straight up in most places. Her clothes are soiled and stained.

"How long have you been wearing that?" I look her up and down.

"Why the hell did you bring *her*?" Amber snaps.

"Watching you come through that door reminds me of the first time I came to get you over twenty years ago. You were young, vibrant, and full of unactualized potential. You're getting old, Amber. Wrinkles are forming around your eyes and mouth and dying your grey hair can no longer conceal your age. When is this going to stop? When will enough be enough?" Aunt Jewel questions.

"You know I didn't call you to listen to this crap!" Amber chimes. "Your *do better* speech hasn't changed anything in all of these years. When are you going to realize that you are wasting your words on deaf ears? I'm starving. Take me to get something to eat," Amber scoffs as she walks toward the door past Aunt Jewel.

We walk to the car in silence. Aunt Jewel turns the ignition and begins to drive. Still, no one says a thing. The radio is even mute. It's a long, silent ride that is quite noisy in the spaces of our minds. Meanwhile, Amber is still prepared for a fight. It's written all over her face and body. She's twitching and moving about in her seat, unable to sit still, the results of long-term drug abuse and the desperate need for a fix. I still can't fathom how I was born from her. I feel dirty every time I think about it. As her body odor fills the car I wonder when she last showered. I roll down the window, but the cold air is biting. I'll just have to try holding my breath until we get home.

Amber looks over to Jewel, breaking the silence. "Thanks for coming to get me. I'll pay you back."

"In the forty plus years we've been on this earth, Amber, you've never paid me back for anything, nor do I expect you to at this point. Besides I wouldn't take it if you tried. I'm going to take you home with us, so you can get yourself cleaned up," Aunt Jewel replies.

Amber quietly says, "Thanks."

Aunt Jewel wins the battle with her silence. Upon arriving home, Amber gets into the shower while Aunt Jewel prepares tea and lays out a change of clothes for her.

"Why do you still help her?" I ask.

"Because she's family and doesn't have anyone else."

"But that's the life she chose. *She* broke all bonds. You don't owe her anything," I say. "And if you left her in there, she'd be forced to sober up."

"There are some things you don't know. There was a time when she needed me but because I was too caught up in myself, I didn't go back for her. Since then, she has never been the same," she admits.

"What happened?" I ask.

"Tonight is a perfect night to have an open discussion with your mother. Maybe it'll help you to understand her better," she says.

"Oh, I understand her plenty. I don't need to know anymore," I say.

"If you knew a little less, you could learn a lot more."

"What does that mean?"

"It means that when you think you know everything, you limit yourself from expanding your knowledge with anything new. There's always more to learn because none of us has it all figured out," she explains.

The bathroom door opens, and Amber comes out.

"Stormey, go to your room for a minute while I talk to your mother," Aunt Jewel requests.

"Gladly." I walk to my room, leaving the door cracked.

Aunt Jewel prays softly, "Father, Mother God. Holy Spirit. Guardian Angels and Ancestors. Open our minds. Fill us with your Spirit. Guide our words. Mend our hearts tonight. Ashe´."

She places the teacups on the table as they sit. "I've always loved how you make your tea with fresh mint leaves," Amber says. She takes a sip, "While I was in the shower a question came to mind that I can't seem to answer. Why do you still show up?"

Aunt Jewel is silent and hesitates to respond. She finally says with sincerity, "You're my baby sister. Being here for you is my duty. I get that now. Unlike before when I left you behind to pursue my own dreams. I thought that chasing the world's idea of success would make me happy, but I realized too late that being able to be here for my family is all I truly need to be happy. I was foolish and wasn't there for you when I should've been. Who you are, what you've become, is because I failed to protect you."

Amber quickly responds, "So it's not because you love me, it's because you feel guilty. You feel responsible for me not living up to who you think I should be."

"I can't help but to feel responsible. Who you are is a direct result of where I failed you. So yes, there's guilt in my heart, but there's also the fear of something happening to you because of me not being there now," Aunt Jewel says.

"You can't change what happened," Amber admits. "I know I told you that it was your fault, but I don't blame you anymore. Hell, it happened to you too. If I would've escaped, I wouldn't have come back either."

Aunt Jewel stirs her tea. "Things are changing and I can't remain the glue that holds everything together anymore. Your daughters need someone in their corner. Amber, when can they count on you to answer their calls?"

Amber's body language instantly changes from open to angry. "What's that supposed to mean? They're grown. They'll be alright. I knew you'd get tired eventually but I never thought you would turn your back on the girls."

Jewel responds, "You're so quick to anger that you don't even hear what I'm saying. I won't be in the position to help much longer, not because I don't want to, but because I won't be able to. I'm telling you because it's time for you to be here for *your girls*. It's time for you to get your life together."

Amber quips, "If it were really that easy, don't you think I would've snapped my fingers and done it already?"

Jewel replies, "Amber, stop feeling sorry for yourself. If you really want to change, you can, and you know it. You don't *want* to change because changing means that you will have to let go. Let go of your excuses and the story you cling to – to feel justified in never moving your life forward. The only reason your past still affects you is because you're holding onto it and carrying it with you everywhere you go. What happened to you is over. Harry is no longer the one hurting you, it's you that is doing the damage now."

"You sit here all self-righteous judging me. You think I like living like this? I have a disease," Amber defends.

"I'm not self-righteous, but I know you are stronger than you think. You were not the only child to suffer from abuse and molestation. We both were violated, so I am not making light of what you went through. I get it. What I don't get is how you're addicted to pain," Jewel answers.

Amber screams, "So what, I'm not as strong as you! Is that what you want to hear?"

Jewel says, "No, it's not. I made a choice to not let those moments define me. I chose to move past it but you chose to stay there. You eat, sleep, and breathe the pain of our childhood. It's been over for thirty years but even today, that man still has a grip on you. You're letting him win."

"And you're free, Jewel? Do you really believe that? If you were so free you wouldn't still be trying to save me. Did you ever think about that?" Amber asks.

Jewel says, "I *am* free because I forgave him a long time ago."

"Forgave him? You are crazier than I thought. He doesn't deserve forgiveness!" Amber yells.

"I didn't forgive him because he deserved it," Jewel says. "I forgave him because I knew that I would never heal until I released the pain. Holding onto anger was causing me to suffer. I learned to use the power of my thinking to see things differently."

I hold my mouth in shock trying not to make a sound.

Aunt Jewel continues, "Thinking back on that experience is no different than thinking about what I had for breakfast this morning. It's not happening anymore. I am safe now. And so are you. You are free, Amber. When are you going to realize that?"

"Yeah, what-eh-ver!" Amber yells.

"Stormey, is that you?" Aunt Jewel calls out after hearing the floorboard in the hallway creak.

Busted. "Yes, I'm going to the bathroom," I say, hoping to be convincing.

"Come sit with us," she requests.

"I'm exhausted. I need to lie down." I hope to avoid whatever is happening between them.

Amber says, "That girl has never liked me, and to be honest, I'm not too fond of her and that nasty attitude either."

Aunt Jewel quickly responds, "She has a reason to be upset with you and you know it."

Amber grows quiet. She stands up and says, "I'm tired as well. I'm going to lay down."

Aunt Jewel stands up visibly upset, "No! Both of you sit down right now! I'm not asking."

I don't recall seeing Aunt Jewel angry before and I surely can't recall her ever yelling. I nervously sit at the table with Amber.

"Now, listen. There's a lot that has been left unsaid between you. As the days have gone on you both have found comfort in the distance. You are not two random women on the street. You're mother and daughter. Whether you admit it or not, there's a bond that can never be broken. Amber, it is time for you to talk to your daughter. Let her know you, that's the only way she can understand."

"Look at her," Amber responds. "She doesn't want to know me. Sitting there looking at me that way. Who do you think you are to look at me like that? You really think you're something, huh? Walking around here with your head filled with dreams. You think I didn't have dreams, too? What makes you think you're any different? You're nothing. Look around. This is reality. This is all life has in store for you. The sooner you get those dreams out of your head the better off you'll be."

I reply, "No, you're mistaken. I came from nothing. This legacy of nothingness that you created stops with you. I'm not like you. I could never allow myself to fall as low as you. No one and nothing will ever hurt me enough that I'll lose focus and give up on myself the way you have. You love your drugs more than you love yourself, more than you love your kids. What kind of woman are you?"

"Stop! Stop it now! What is wrong with the both of you? This is ridiculous. Why must you spit venom and use your tongues as weapons?" Aunt Jewel questions.

"Aunt Jewel, I'm sorry but I can't sit and talk with her. There is nothing that she can say that will ever make me understand how she could do the things she's done," I say.

"Nobody has done anything to you! With your ol' cry baby self," Amber says.

"You were so caught up in your mess that you never noticed Pete watching me like I was a piece of meat to be devoured. Thank God Jay heard my screams and came when he did. Who knows what would have happened to me," I say.

"What are you talking about Stormey?" Aunt Jewel asks.

"Pete, our former landlord, tried to rape me the day you came and got me from that God-forsaken-place."

"You're full of it! I don't have to sit here and listen to these lies," Amber demands. She stands up and grabs her coat.

"Where are you going? Amber, hear her out," Aunt Jewel states.

"I can't sit here and listen to anymore of her lies. I need to get out of here." Amber opens the front door.

"Amber don't leave. It's late and it's cold."

"Look, I'm a grown woman and I don't have to answer to anyone about how I live my life. And I'm surely not going to sit here listening to her lying all night."

"Don't come back!" I yell as I rise out of my chair and quickly slam the door in her face. I'm not sure what Aunt Jewel thought was going to happen tonight. We are the same as we've always been, broken.

CHAPTER 16

Stroke of Midnight

"Ugh, this day couldn't go any slower!" I impatiently stare down the clock.

Bree looks up from a magazine and says, "Girl, chill. You only have an hour left before you're off into the sunset with your boo."

I laugh because she's right. Usually I don't mind working. In fact, I actually enjoy it. Bree and I get along well, which makes the days go by easy. Today is different, though. It's Valentine's Day and Ace is picking me up when I get off. It's our first Valentine's Day together and I can't help but to let my thoughts wonder on what he has planned for us. In all honesty, I'm excited just to spend the evening with him.

As I'm wiping down tables, an older man in his forties comes inside the diner wearing a black trench coat over a black suit with a white shirt, a black bow tie, and fancy shoes, looking as if he's stumbled upon the wrong neighborhood.

He approaches Bree at the register. "I'm looking for Stormey."

My heart ticks a bit faster; I don't know what business this man could possibly have with me. He pulls out a small black box with a red ribbon tied in a bow and says, "I have a special delivery. Which of you lovely ladies is Stormey?"

"I am," I say hesitantly.

The gentleman hands me the box and says, "Ace sent me. This is from him."

I happily receive it, he smiles and exits the store. Bree jumps up from leaning on the counter, "What is it?"

"I don't know," I answer.

She eagerly says, "What are you waiting for? Open it!"

I slowly and anxiously untie the ribbon. Bree is standing so close that I can feel her breath on my face. As excited as she is, you'd think it was something for us both. I take a step back and pull the lid off slowly. Inside is a small white card folded in half. It has a hand-written message. *Sorry, I can't pick you up tonight. My mom needs me to handle some things at the salon. The driver will bring you to me.*

Before I can fully process the message, Bree runs to the door and screams, "Oh my God, girl! There's a limo out here. I cannot believe this! You're so lucky. You must've finally let him knock them cobwebs off that thang and you didn't even tell me!"

I giggle and calmly walk to the door. A classic white Rolls Royce Excalibur Stretch Limousine sits in the lot. I'm excited but don't want to show it too much. I walk back to the counter. "I haven't given up anything. He's just romantic."

Bree looks at me in disbelief, following behind me. "Either you're lying or you're the luckiest girl in the world. Either way, he's a keeper."

"He always makes me feel special. They say there aren't any good guys out there but I found one."

Bree says, "At least it appears that way."

I'm not sure if she's throwing shade, but I ignore her comment as I fantasize about what's coming next. When the clock strikes six, I immediately grab my belongings and hurry to the door.

"Dang, thirsty!" Bree says. "You better call and tell me every detail!"

"I will. Promise." I step outside and the driver is standing with his hands folded, looking official. He opens the rear door of the limo and holds it as I get inside. I can't believe my eyes. There are flower bouquets everywhere; it looks and smells like heaven! On the seat is another black box with a red ribbon with my name on it, just like the one I received earlier. Inside, another handwritten message.

> *I selected each of these flowers because they represent attributes of you.*
> *The lilies embody our friendship and devotion.*
> *Gardenias express your purity and innocence.*
> *Hydrangeas personify your enduring grace and beauty.*
> *The gladiolas signify your moral strength and integrity.*
> *Tulips represent our perfect love.*
> *Last but not least, Sunflowers (your favorite) are known for their longevity; I wish that for us.*

My eyes water as I literally melt into the seat reading his words. I'm honored to be thought of this way especially by someone I adore just the same. Overwhelmed with joy, I can't help but to cry. I've never felt so loved and adored. I move to the back of the limo to smell each flower arrangement. I've smelled flowers before, but today it's like I'm smelling their fragrance for the first time.

After driving thirty minutes or so, the limo stops and I immediately wipe my face and gather my composure. I look out and see a sign that reads, *The Diamond Experience*. The driver opens the door for me. I step out and he escorts me to the salon entrance and opens the door.

I walk, yet it feels more like I'm floating. I look around and am surprised at how beautiful everything is. It's not what I was expecting. Ace always referred to his mother's business as a salon, but it's more like a spa. The place is huge with multiple stations and private rooms tending to different services such as hair, nails, makeup, facials, body treatments, and massages. A young, attractive lady wearing all black stands at the counter.

She interrupts my gaze of amazement and says, "Do you have an appointment?"

I reply, "No, I'm here to see Ace. Could you let him know I'm here?"

She smiles, "You must be Stormey."

"I am."

She walks out from behind the counter and says, "Come with me."

I follow behind her as she leads me to a stylist and says, "Stormey's here."

The stylist says, "I'm Jade, Ace's sister. It's nice to finally meet you. Ace stepped out but I'll be taking care of you. Would you like anything to drink? We have champagne, wine, tea, coffee, and water."

"I'm okay. Thank you."

Jade turns to another woman. "Candace, your appointment is here."

"Appointment?" I ask.

Jade says, "Ace booked a spa day for you. Your job is to sit back and relax for the next couple of hours. You can start by picking a color for your nails."

I pick a pink nude nail polish.

Candace says, "I'm going to do your pedicure first." She leads me to the pedicure station with large leather massaging chairs and a pulsating foot bath. I sit in the chair while soaking my feet. It feels so good. After she finishes my pedicure, she gives me a hot paraffin wax treatment and manicure on my hands and leaves me to sit for a few minutes while my nails dry.

Jade returns and directs me to the shampoo bowl where she washes my hair. She says, "Today, you're getting the royal treatment. Relax and take it all in."

I take her advice and close my eyes and enjoy the moment.

"My brother must really think you're special. This is the first time he's ever asked me to do this for anyone."

I don't really know how to respond, so I don't.

She continues, "He has something special planned for you tonight."

I respond, "Really? Did he tell you what?"

"Yes, but he swore me to secrecy. He gets his romantic ways from our dad who used to always say it was the man's responsibility to plan and prove himself to a woman that's worthy. All she should have to do is show up."

"Well, Ace had a great teacher because I've yet to be disappointed." Ace outdoes himself at every turn and has given me the best experiences of my life. I can't believe they're doing all of this for me.

"Your hair is so beautiful and thick."

"Thank you. My hair bun is bit deceitful." She blows it dry, flat irons it, then pins it up while leaving some of the hair hanging down to make tendrils. I stare at myself in the mirror. "I love it. I've never seen my hair look so elegant!"

"Wait until you see your makeup." She signals Zoey to come back.

This just keeps getting better. I feel like a little kid on Christmas morning. Each gift I open is even more exciting than the last. I do my own makeup all the time but to have it done professionally makes me feel important like a celebrity or something. She dusts on foundation and gives me lightly blushed cheeks with a nude lip. She dresses my eyes with shadow, liner, and lashes.

She turns me around to face the mirror. "I look flawless."

Jade return with a box with a red bow. "Ready for your next experience?"

I surprisingly ask, "There's more?"

She smiles and says, "Come with me."

I follow her again, this time to a room in the back. She hands me the box and says, "Go on the other side of the partition and change into this."

Before I can respond, she leaves. I untie the bow and open the box. Inside is another handwritten note. *Put this on. The driver will take you to your next destination.*

Inside is a beautiful, elegant, floor-length black lace dress with long sleeves. It's see-through everywhere except the bodice. The back has small crystal buttons running the length of the dress and there is a pair of sparkling high heels covered in black crystals. I put everything on, and of course, it all fits perfectly.

I ask Jade, "Would you mind helping me with the buttons?"

"Of course," she answers while looking me over. "You should see yourself. Come over here to the mirror."

I lift the bottom of my dress and when we get to the mirror, I am in awe of my reflection. "I feel like I belong on the red carpet."

Overwhelmed with joy, I begin to cry. I inhale deeply through my nose and hold my head back to keep my tears from falling. Ace has far surpassed my Valentine's Day expectations. I feel happy and sad at the same time because I almost feel like I don't deserve it. Not in my entire life, nor in my grandest dreams, has anyone loved me like this, nor have I ever looked so amazing. Nothing compares to how I feel right now so I soak it all in. This is the kind of love Aunt Jewel told me to wait for. The kind of love that comes without reason and reminds me that I am worthy because I am here, and I am me.

I walk out of the salon totally transformed. The driver opens the limo door and we drive to the next destination. This time the note doesn't say where we're going. I reread the note that came with the flowers. I allow myself to fantasize about what Ace has up his sleeve next. When the limo stops I look out of the window to see we are in the Art Village.

I step out and the driver says, "This way, Miss," as he escorts me to the entrance of the art gallery.

He opens the door and as I walk in, I immediately feel comforted and at home. I love this gallery. The shiny hardwood floors, the large open spaces, and the magnificent creations all around me make me secretly wish I could move in. I absolutely love it here.

I look around and realize that no one else is here. The driver takes my coat and I take in the low lighting. Right before he exits the building he says, "Enjoy your evening."

I walk in the direction of the soft music playing that sounds like a string instrument. My eyes glance at the beautiful art surrounding me but then, I see Ace standing in the middle of the gallery, patiently waiting with his hands folded in front of him. He's wearing an all-black tuxedo with a bow tie and shiny black shoes.

Next to him is a violinist. I look him in his eyes, he smiles, and I fall into his embrace. He is like a magnet that tugs at my soul. For a moment I stay in his arms because the pull is too strong to break. He must feel it as well because he's holding me in the most sensual way and I don't want it to end.

"Good evening, Princess. You look beautiful." He gently releases me from his arms and pulls out a chair while gesturing for me to sit down. I hadn't even noticed the table that was set for dinner.

I look at the menu and to my surprise it reads, *Stormey's Knight* in large cursive letters. I chuckle at the play on words, wondering if he thinks he's my knight. The menu shows that we're having a seven-course meal!

I look up to see Ace on the phone. "We're ready," he says and hangs up.

I'm curious so I say, "Who was that?"

He smiles. "You'll see."

A moment later, a man wearing black chef attire walks towards us with a platter. He serves the first course, Oysters Rockefeller. I look at Ace and say, "This looks amazing! What is it? Annnd how do I eat it?"

Ace laughs and shows me how. As I dip the oysters in butter and sample them, my palette seems to come to life. "These are amazing."

"I'm glad you like them. They're almost as amazing as you," he flirts causing me to blush.

Next, the chef serves Lobster Bisque as the second course. "This is so delicious. I've never had bisque, but I am sure this is the most amazing soup ever." I look up to find Ace staring at me endearingly. I look into his eyes and smile.

For the third course the chef serves baby greens with candied shallots, strawberries, and roasted pecans tossed in a vinaigrette. Each bite is simply mouthwatering. Ace and I continue to eat while gazing into each other's eyes as the chef serves us garlic roasted shrimp cocktail for the fourth course.

"Being in an art museum is so inspiring. I hope to one day create something worthy of being displayed among these masterpieces," I say.

"You're already worthy. Everyone else will soon know it." Ace leans over to kiss my hand. I can't stop staring intensely in his eyes. He winks at me and I realize how deeply I am falling in love with this man. I knew he cared for me, but today I feel like he loves me too. I'm nervous about falling for him because I still don't know what his plans are. Who will he choose to listen to, Rich or Tone?

I'm afraid to say anything because I don't want to ruin this perfect night but I can't allow myself to fall any further without knowing. "I haven't heard you mention the wash in a while. Is everything okay?"

"Yes, I took a few days off to clear my head."

"Is there anything you need to talk about?"

"Nah, I just got a few things to work out, but nothing major."

"Have you heard from Rich lately?

"Stormey, let's focus on us tonight." I nod to agree.

The fifth course is a large serving spoon with a curved handle and a dollop of lemon sorbet. The chef reads my facial expression and says, "It is to cleanse the palette before eating the main course. I will be back momentarily."

The violinist continues to play beautiful serenades, amplifying everything I am feeling, but I can't move forward without knowing where Ace stands. "I don't want to distract from tonight, but I know about the phone and I want to know what your plans are because I'm falling for you and I don't want to fall too deep if you are planning on doing business with Rich. You know that's a deal breaker for me."

"Well, you don't have to worry. I had a heart-to-heart with my uncle and had some time to think about what he said. I'm not cut out for what I was planning. The risk is too great and the consequences are too severe."

"I'm so relieved to hear you say that," I gush.

"Now can we focus on this moment?"

I can't keep the smile off my face. "Absolutely." The main course consists of seared scallops with lemon and garlic pan sauce. "The food is so delicious that I can barely speak."

"Wait until you try this, crème caramel. Mmmmm," Ace says.

"I'm stuffed but cannot resist eating every last bite."

As the chef and his staff clean up, Ace stands and reaches his hand out to me. I place my hand in his and he gently pulls me into him. We lock eyes as he holds me. As we sway to the music, an all-consuming passion burns within me. I am experiencing something that only happens in fairy tales, but this is not make-believe. This is my real life. He looks at me with enchanting eyes as we dance cheek to cheek.

I realize the music has stopped and we are dancing in silence. I look up and notice the driver is holding my coat. When Ace looks his way, he taps his watch. Ace gently grabs my hand and whispers, "It's time."

I ask him, "Time for what?" as the driver assists me with my coat.

He says softly, "Your fairy godmother has requested that you be home before the stroke of midnight, My Princess."

Ace and I walk out to the limo. The driver holds the door as we climb into the back amongst the flower arrangements. I look at Ace and cannot imagine going home. I am not ready for the night to end. This day has been perfect.

I lean in to kiss Ace softly and say, "Tonight has been a dream come true. As with all fairy tales, the guy gets the girl. Take me to your palace, Prince Charming."

Ace looks surprised. He says softly, "That's not what this is about."

I could not imagine any time being more perfect than this moment. I place my hand onto his as I gaze at him and say, "I didn't know until I knew, but this is the moment I have been waiting for."

"Okay!" He calls the driver and says, "Change in plans. Take us to my place."

I lean over and softly place my lips on his. He lifts me from my seat and pulls me into him. His kisses are loving and sensual. Then the limo comes to a stop and the door opens. We step out and Ace lifts me in the air and carries me inside.

CHAPTER 17

Light in the Night

I'm lying in bed staring at the ceiling in disbelief that I'm no longer a virgin. I don't know why I expected to feel *different*; I feel the same as I did yesterday.

"Stormey, hey Stormey, are you still sleep?" Ace whispers.

I open my eyes to see him standing in front of me smiling, holding a tray with something that smells delicious. "Is that coffee?"

"I made you breakfast," he says proudly.

"No one ever served me breakfast in bed before." I excitedly sit up for him to place the tray on my lap. The plate is full of pancakes, eggs, bacon, toast, and a glass of orange juice. The tray is garnished with a single red rose.

Ace kisses me on my forehead and says, "I'll be right back." A few minutes later, he darts back into the bedroom with the biggest smile on his face. He eagerly reaches out for my hand and says, "Come with me. I have something I want to show you."

With a mouthful of egg, I say, "Hold on. I've barely eaten."

He removes the tray from my lap and says, "That can wait. Come on." He grabs my hand and pulls me up from the bed. "Now close your eyes. It's a surprise."

"Come on! Another surprise?" I complain, but I close my eyes anyway as he eagerly leads me out of the bedroom and down the hallway. We come to a quick pause.

"Okay. You can open your eyes now."

We are in a spare bedroom except it's not furnished for that purpose. My mouth drops open as I glance around the room. I am astounded. Against one wall is a long, soft, comfortable couch. In the middle of the room is a drafting desk typically used by artists. Against an adjacent wall is a storage compartment with several see-through drawers. I look inside the drawers and find they're filled with every supply an artist could ever need-paint, chalk, pencils, charcoal, and brushes. The closet space is transformed into a flat storage space with shelves that hold canvases, papers, and other large objects. An easel sits in the corner with a chair placed in front of it.

Ace anxiously utters, "I made you a studio. Now you have somewhere to escape from the world to do what makes you happy."

My mouth gapes open. I place my hands on his cheeks and pull his face into mine. I kiss him madly. He raises me off my feet and he carries me back to the bedroom. On our way, I hear my cell phone ringing. I allow it to go to voicemail since I do not want to stifle this affair, but the phone rings again.

I sigh with disbelief, "Ugh, who keeps calling?"

Ace responds, "Let it ring."

"Hold up. It might be important." I pick it up too late and the call goes to voicemail. Looking at the screen, I notice that I missed eight calls from Aunt Jewel. My chest tightens as my breath becomes heavy. I immediately assume something is severely wrong.

"I really hope everything is okay," I utter as I call her back. Surprisingly, my mother answers. "I see I missed several calls, is everything okay?" I ask nervously.

Amber is frantic. I cannot make out anything she's saying.

"Wait, slow down. What are you saying?" I interject.

Amber repeats herself slowly. "Jewel was admitted into the hospital. She passed out today and I don't know what's wrong with her, but you need to get here *now*."

"When did this happen? How long has she been there?" Before she can respond, I say, "I'm on my way!"

I turn to Ace. "I have to go to the hospital."

Without hesitation, he responds, "I'll take you."

We arrive and I frantically scurry down the hall. I see medical personnel leaving her room. "What's wrong with her, Doctor? Is she going to be okay?"

He answers in a somber tone, "The malignant cancer cells have spread aggressively and now the scans are showing they are present in her brain, too. When she came in she was in severe pain. We gave her painkillers, but they have not eased her condition. She has just been given a sedative. You should hurry in to see her while she is still coherent."

"*Cancer*?" I say shocked. I stare at the door afraid to walk in. I am trying to digest the fact that she has cancer and never told me. I did not know what I would see on the other side of the door.

Ace interrupts my thoughts, "Stormey, you should go in before she falls asleep. That medicine will put her out for a while."

I know he's right. I fight back tears by taking a deep breath and walk inside. Aunt Jewel's eyes light up. "Hey, Darling."

Amber interjects, "It sure did take you long enough." She looks Ace up and down and snarls, "I see you were out with that boy when Jewel needed you at home."

Aunt Jewel says, "Amber, stop it. You're not being fair. Stormey didn't know about my condition. Besides, I don't expect her to stop living her life on account of anyone, not even me." Aunt Jewel looks at me and apologetically says, "I hope you didn't cancel any plans to be here. I don't know why your mother makes such a big fuss about things."

I walk over and wrap my arms around her. "Aunt Jewel, you know I would drop anything for you. Stop being so modest. We love you. We're supposed to make a fuss about things like this."

"I got here as soon as I could." Skye walks in with Troy and goes straight to Aunt Jewel to hug and give her a kiss on the cheek.

Aunt Jewel says, "I was waiting for you."

Skye says, "What happened, Auntie? And don't tell me you're just dehydrated again."

I nod my head. "The jig is up, Auntie. The doctor just told me that you have cancer. Why haven't you said anything?"

"When were you going to tell us?" Skye exclaims.

She hesitates, then says, "I was hoping to be the one to break the news to everybody."

"When was that going to be? You clearly have known about this for a while and chose not to tell any of us," I respond.

"It's not the easiest conversation to have. Besides, I was trying my best to help us bury the past and come together as a family. I wanted us to be at peace, but that moment never came, and my health couldn't hold up any longer, so here we are."

"What on earth would make you think that you could bring us together in peace? If that's what you were waiting on then you never intended on telling us," I said angrily.

"That's enough from you! Nobody has time for that should've, would've, could've crap," Amber interjects.

"Why is it that the people who ought to die, outlive us all?" I snap back.

"Stormey!" Aunt Jewel exclaims, "Now, I know you are upset, but that does not justify your behavior. I'm sorry I didn't say anything sooner, but when was I supposed to tell you? Was I supposed to yell over you, Skye, and Amber screaming at each other? Or after you've come home gushing over Ace? Would either of those have been appropriate times? I hoped I could get all of us in a room together, acting like civilized human beings, or at the very least, have a shell of a family. Apparently, the only thing that can do that is tragedy."

"How long have you known?" Skye asks.

"I found out just before I was admitted into the hospital the last time. I was already into the final stage and it was too aggressive to treat. I told the doctors I'd rather fully live out my last days than be sick from chemo. We knew it was inevitable," she says.

"I knew something wasn't right. You drink too much tea to be dehydrated. I shouldn't have accepted that answer, I just never thought you would lie to us," Skye says.

"I'm sorry, Sweetheart, but I knew what was coming and I needed time to process it myself. I wasn't ready to tell you."

"I just don't understand why you kept this from me, of all people," I say angrily. "I eat meals with you, we sit and talk every single day. How could you not have found a good time to tell me before now? Any time would've been a good time."

Amber adds, "It sounds like you just gave up and decided on your own that you were done trying. This is so selfish of you. Why would you do this?"

"It's no longer about *trying* to live. My cancer is too aggressive for the medicine, so I decided I'd rather have the quality of life I desire instead of being sick and miserable with whatever time I have left."

"How do you know it's too aggressive for the medicine when you haven't even tried it?" Amber demands.

"The doctors and I have been over my options and this is the best decision," she responds.

"You're talking crazy, Auntie! We are not just going to watch you die! You're going to get chemo and we will not hear any more of this crazy talk from you!" Skye states.

"Yeah, Auntie. She's right," I insist. "Since when have you been a quitter? It's not like you to just give up like this. You would never let me accept defeat and I won't allow you. I'm going to call that doctor back in here and he's going to give you the medicine and you're going to get better. I'll call him now."

I reach over her to press the "call nurse" button on her bed. She grabs my hand to stop me. "The doctors have run every test possible, but this disease did not show signs until it was already too late. What's done by God cannot be undone by man, it's my time and I accept it. I lived the life I wanted to live. I look back and I celebrate how far I've come. This is not a moment of sadness, but one of completion. You may not understand it, but please stop fighting and embrace it with me," she pleads.

As she speaks, her eyes fall equally upon Skye, Amber, and me. We are quiet, trying to come to terms with the reality of this situation. She musters up strength as she smiles sweetly at each one of us. She looks at Amber and says, "No matter how far you go it will never be too far, there is always a way back. You may have forgotten who you are, but if you search your heart you will find that you never left, you were just buried beneath the pain. Don't run from it because you have to dig through it to rise to the surface once again."

She reaches out and touches Skye's hand. "Skye, my feisty go-getter. All the riches that you desire are within your reach, but you are reaching in the wrong direction. You are destined to have everything your heart desires, but you will never find your treasure because you are searching the earth for what is already in your soul. Someday soon, you will see it for yourself."

"Auntie stop it," I say as tears stream down my cheeks. "Stop talking like that. I don't want to hear it. I can't think about losing you. You're my light, my air. How can I see without you? How can I breathe?"

"Stormey, I was never your light," she whispers. "I'm only a mirror that's been reflected back to you. The light that you see is and always has been your own. The world may seem like it's consumed by darkness, but you have to bring the light from within you out into the world. You will forever be consumed with darkness until you decide to be the light in the night. Once you do, you will see that there are others who will shine with you. You will never be alone," she says.

Aunt Jewel smiles and in the sweetest and most heartfelt voice she says, "No matter what happens we will always be family. That will never change."

She pauses. "We're all just doing the best we know how. Don't be too hard on each other. Life is complicated. It's not easy for anyone, but what matters most is how you treat the people you share your journey with. Don't get so caught up in your pursuit of things that you end up with nothing at all. The relationships you build are what fills you up."

She looks around the room with a light in her eyes. She glows with love illuminating from deep within. "Stormey and Skye, the house is paid for and both of your names are on the deed. You two will always have a place to live and my attorney, Justin Starks, will be in touch to go over my will when the time comes."

Even as she is laying there fighting for her life, she's still taking care of us. That's who she is, the comforter. Her presence alone told us that no matter what, everything was always okay. She gave our shared blood meaning; she was the only link keeping us together.

I don't know if I am angry or distraught. I want to scream at her, but the respect I have for her won't let me. So, I cry. My tears make it okay for everyone else in the room to cry as well. We all cry together as Auntie closes her eyes. A long and steady beep emitting from the heart monitor silences our sobbing. Aunt Jewel lays quietly, looking like she's sleeping peacefully, but the machine tells a different story.

It doesn't feel real. I feel myself being escorted out of the room in a hurry as the medical team rushes in to offer life-saving techniques. I look back at her as they close the door. Her body lying motionless tells me that her soul left her body while we were locked in our grief, crying.

The only consolation is that she finally had us all in the same room together. She said what she needed to say to each of us. I know what the doctor is going to say before he says it. I sit silently as they talk to Amber and Skye. I watch as they hold each other and cry.

As I walk toward the exit, Ace walks up and grabs my hand. I want to wake up but realize this isn't a bad dream, it's a living nightmare. "I never imagined she would die, not like this, not this soon. She's been the only person that ever believed in me...believed I was worth anything. The only person I knew I could trust. Because of her, my heart had finally healed, only to be shattered all over again."

"Stormey, I know this is hard. I'm here for you," Ace reassures me.

"I know, but I want to be alone right now," I reply.

"I understand. Where do you want me to take you?"

"I want to walk for a while. I'll call you later."

"Okay, don't hesitate to let me know if you need anything."

It's pouring down when I arrive home. The rain hits me hard, drenching me, but I'm so numb I barely notice. Tears slowly stream down my face and sorrow sets in heavily. I try to stay positive about my life, but it seems like no matter what I do to stay afloat, there is always something weighing me down. I keep getting hit by waves knocking me back down. Now a tsunami.

I don't know how much more I can take before drowning in it all. I don't understand why things get better temporarily, just to get worse again. Or why my entire existence has been nothing more than various degrees of suffering. Why does life tease me with possibilities only to never make good on any of them?

Aunt Jewel always talked to me about God and I prayed for Him to change the circumstances in my life for the better. But better never came and now I am angrier than ever!

As I stand at the porch steps in the pouring rain, I hesitate to go inside. I can hardly breathe because I know Aunt Jewel won't be inside. I purposely knock over a geranium pot. Then I pick up a second one and throw it against the house.

My mascara runs all over my face and I can barely see. I cry and scream, not caring who can hear me or who might see me. I yell at the sky because I cannot find the words I need to curse the God Aunt Jewel taught me to pray to. I scream from every pore in my body, crying out with the agony of my soul to the heavens. I dare Him to ignore me. I scream so loud I'm sure that God's ears hurt. I hope to remind Him that I exist. I scream until I can't belt out anything more than a squeal.

Satisfied that God felt my wrath, I walk to the door and insert my key. The house is completely dark. My eyes stare into the kitchen and I quickly remember the countless conversations we had while sitting at the table while I helped her cook. I sit in the chair that I would normally sit in and let the memories play in my mind like a movie. I want to hear her voice again. There is so much I need to hear from her right now. I pick up my cell and call her phone repeatedly, letting it ring just to hear her voice on her voicemail. I want to talk to her so badly that I leave a message hoping she will somehow receive it.

"I miss you, and it hurts so much. I don't know how you stayed so positive in a relentless world. I never saw you suffer, not even in death. I don't know what to do without you here to guide me. You were my everything, my guardian angel. You gave me your light of love, mercy, and grace and I never thanked you. I never had anyone in my corner like you. There's no one here to tell me things are going to get better. I hope you can hear me tonight because I need you more than ever right now. I would give anything to hear you encourage me one more time. I just feel so..."— *beep! your recording has reached its maximum length. To replay your message—*

I throw my phone across the room and cry out. I walk to my bedroom to take off my rain-soaked clothes. I fall onto the floor landing on my knees. It strikes me at my core, I am alone. Again. Without her here I have no one to call, no one to lean on. She was the one person that I thought I could always count on. I cry uncontrollably until my body curls into a ball on the floor.

CHAPTER 18

Repercussions

The sun has fallen into its slumber, much like me. The sun has set on my joy, shattering my wishes, hopes, and dreams for the future. Each day has been long, harsh, and bitter. Since Aunt Jewel died, I've been sulking in bed, not wanting to face anyone. I've barely even gotten up for food or water. Although Ace has been here by my side, nothing feels the same because I just keep waiting for Aunt Jewel to walk through the front door and tell me it was all a bad dream.

There's so much for me to figure out and I don't even know where to begin. I hate feeling like this but I can't pull myself out of this funk. I don't want to pray or meditate. I don't want to read or think good thoughts. I just want to brood. Sulking is the only thing that feels easy.

I roll over to check my phone and there hasn't been one call or text. There are so many people in the world that it's practically overcrowded, yet on this sad day, it feels like no one cares. It's ironic how there are over a billion people in the world, but each one of us is so self-absorbed that we don't take notice of the person next to us. I was living with my aunt, yet I never noticed she was sick or dying. How messed up is that? I was so blinded by my pettiness that I never noticed she was losing weight and more tired than normal. I now reap my own karma as I lay unnoticed, wondering if I died right now, would anyone care? If I did, then maybe I could see Auntie again.

I force myself out of bed to answer a knock on my door.

"I've been calling you all morning, why haven't you answered?" Ace says anxiously.

"That's strange. My phone didn't ring."

"Well, get dressed. Black is on his way here to see you. He said it's urgent."

"Urgent? What on earth could he want with me?"

"I'm not sure, you know how Black is. He never gives a straight answer." Ace wraps his arms around me and squeezes me tight. He whispers in my ear, "Stormey, you need to take a shower. It'll make you feel better."

"Is that your nice way of telling me I smell?" I joke.

"Well, you may be a little tart. Just a little," he gestures by creating a small space between his thumb and index finger, then he laughs.

"Forget you," I chuckle and push him away.

I step into the shower. The hot water feels good against my body. I move in closer and close my eyes, so it pours onto my face. Listening to the sound of each drop splashing in the tub reminds me of rain. My thoughts drift and I don't bother to stop them.

"Stormey! You alright in there?" Ace breaks me out of my trance.

"Yeah. I'm fine."

"Black is here."

"I'll be right out." As I get dressed, my thoughts race while I speculate about what Black wants. After I walk into the room, I feel an eeriness in the air. Black sits on the couch talking on the phone. Ace is sitting quietly with a worried look in his eyes. He's making me nervous. I sit on the other couch.

Black says, "It's your sister."

My breath becomes heavy and my chest rises with each inhale. He did not have to say anything more because I already knew. "What did Troy do to her?"

"Hold on," he says to the person on the phone. Then he reaches over and says, "It's Skye."

I'm confused as I take the phone from him. "Hello?"

"Why haven't you been answering your phone? I've been trying to call you all day," she says.

"I must've forgotten to pay my bill with everything that's been going on." Here I was being dramatic thinking no one cared about me and it was my error the whole time.

"Well you need to take care of that ASAP because I'm going to be calling you again."

"The person you are talking to is in a Correctional Facility. This call may be monitored and recorded..." the automated recording warns.

"You're in jail? Why are you in jail?"

"Troy got me caught up. He asked me to give him a ride across town and when we got to the spot, he told me to wait in the car. He went into an apartment building and came back out a few minutes later carrying a duffle bag. He put the bag in the trunk and got into the car."

"What does this have to do with you being in jail?" I interrupt.

"When we were on our way back to the house, the police blew down on us. The officer said we didn't use our turn signal, but I used it. I think they were watching us," she says.

"Get to the part about how you ended up in jail?"

"The officer walked his K-9 around the car and it picked up on something in the trunk. They checked and found what Troy had in the duffle bag and arrested us both."

"Well, what was in the bag?" I ask.

"They said it was heroin," she answers.

"HEROIN!"

"What's really messed up is that Troy immediately started playing crazy, like he didn't know what was in the bag or how it got in the trunk. He even went as far as to tell the officer that he was only getting a ride because his license was suspended," she continues.

"That lowlife, dirty dog! I told you he didn't love you! I told you to leave him before he destroyed you! I can't believe this! Did you tell them the truth?" I rant.

"Yes, I told them, but it doesn't look good because the car is in my name and I was driving, so they say I'm responsible regardless. The only way I can get out of it is if he confesses. I can't believe he's such a coward to let me go through this knowing that I didn't do anything but give him a ride. I heard of women catching cases running with dudes that slang, but I never thought it could happen to me. He didn't even hesitate to turn on me. I could face some serious time. I thought he loved me, but now I see he only cares about himself," she says.

"This is messed up, Skye. This is really messed up. So, what now? What's going to happen to you?" I ask.

"They charged both of us with trafficking and at this point it's my word against his, so we have to wait until the trial to sort it out. In the meantime, I'm going to figure out a way to expose the truth, but I can't do nothing from inside here. Black is going to give you some money. Find Momma and get her down here to post my bond," she says.

"Find Momma? Why? If Black has the money, why can't he do it?"

"He doesn't want to put his name on anything. I can't blame him, I'm just grateful that he's willing to put up the money to get me out," she says.

"*You have 15 seconds remaining on this call,*" the automated recording warns.

"I'll do it," I offer.

"Okay cool. I need to get out of here ASAP," she replies.

"I'm on my way," I say just before the call disconnects. I hand Black his phone back. "Ugh! I told her not to trust him. I knew he would ruin her!"

"Yeah, according to your sister, Troy was doing business with an undercover and once he left the meeting spot they trailed him and arrested them both," Black explains.

"An undercover? She didn't mention anything about that."

"Look, I just came by to give you this money. She can tell you whatever she wants you to know once she gets out," Black says.

"Troy is a snake. I can't believe she was so stupid to mess with him. I always knew he was trouble since the first day she brought him around. It's obvious that anyone who sells drugs doesn't have a soul. Why did she think he was any different?"

"You can hold all of that down, acting all high and mighty!" Black snaps.

"I never *have* and never *will* date a drug dealer. And I surely wouldn't be stupid enough to wind up in jail because of a selfish bastard like Troy. If that makes me high and mighty then so be it!" I snap back.

"You can't be serious. I don't know if you're delusional or really that naïve. She's in jail because of herself. She chose this lifestyle when she wanted the goods that only drug money can afford. This is part of the game. Old boy messed up by getting greedy with someone he didn't know. Now they're paying the consequences for being reckless. She's not innocent and neither are you. You're enjoying the fruits of drug money because Ace was raised on it and everything his father left him came from it," Black declares.

"Ace is not his father!" I argue.

Black chuckles to himself, "Ace, this girl is funny. Is she really this stupid?"

"Chill out Dude, don't talk about her like that," Ace says.

"Who are you calling stupid?" I scold. "I'm far from stupid. Ace makes his money at the car wash and works hard for what he has, something you don't know anything about."

Black laughs even harder, "Maaaan, get yo girl before I do."

"Dude, chill. What are you on right now? We have more important things to focus on anyway," Ace states.

"Like what?"

"Like this." Ace pulls a phone out of his pocket. "Remember when I met up with Rich the other day?"

"Yeah, what about it?" Black asks.

"He gave me this," he shows Black the phone. "Look at these messages."

"What is this?"

"Read it! It says, *hurry up and get in position he's heading out of the diner. King must die tonight.* Period."

"Do you know whose phone this is?" Black looks pale, as if all the blood has left his body.

"Nah, this obviously belongs to whoever shot my dad. But more importantly, I need to know who ordered the hit."

"So all you have is a phone with a message? How is that supposed to help?" Black asks.

Ace presses the call button and says, "Maybe you'll recognize their voice when they answer."

Immediately, a phone rings inside Black's pocket. The phone goes to voicemail. Ace calls it back again and the phone in Black's pocket rings again.

"You have another phone?" Ace asks.

Black yells, "Are you kidding me right now?"Ace hangs up and calls the phone back again. The phone in Black's pocket rings again. "This is you?" Ace questions confused.

Black laughs uncontrollably, appearing to have some sort of psychotic break as he yells, "This what you want!" He steps back, pulls out a black semi-automatic handgun and points it at Ace. "You and your father are just alike – weak."

"You're going to shoot me? Just like that you're going to take my life?" Ace nervously backs away.

Black points his gun at Ace. "I wasn't even mentioned in his will. I'm his first born and even in his death I don't matter."

"That doesn't have anything to do with me." Ace declares.

"It has everything to do with you."

"I didn't do anything to you. That was between you and my father," Ace responds.

Black chuckles, "*Your father?* See, that's exactly why I don't regret a damn thing I did to take the throne."

"It was you the whole time. You were the one that set him up?" Ace shouts as he steps toward Black.

Black swings at Ace and hits him in the head with the butt of his gun. Ace falls onto the floor upon impact.

"Oh, you're walking up empty-handed to a gun. You bad, huh?" Black taunts.

"Stop!" I scream.

Ace holds his bleeding head, "Did you do it? Did you kill him?"

"Nah, I didn't. He eliminated himself the day he chose you and your mother over me and mines. It was only a matter of time before it came back to bite him," Black states. "I was patient. Until I wasn't."

"He was your father, too! He may not have been perfect, but he kept you under his wing and showed you everything he knew about the streets. He's the reason you are in the position you are. Apparently, none of that means anything to you. You had him killed because he didn't choose you and your mother? Is that what you're telling me? How could you?"

"How could I? How could I *not*? He was never a father to me! Was he my mentor in this game? Yes. Father? No. He was *your father*, not mine. Every day I was around, you two made it clear. He called you son and called me his protege. He chose you over me and I chose the game over him. I saw my opportunity to become The King and I took it. It wasn't personal, it was business," Black explains.

I was in shock from all that I was hearing, and terrified because if he was saying this out loud, he didn't have any intentions of letting either of us walk out of here alive. "Black, please stop. You're just upset. Calm down before you do something you'll regret later."

"Regret? I don't have regrets," Black says to me.

Ace jumps up and charges Black, attempting to grab the gun. "You think it's that easy? You think I'm just going to let you kill me?" Ace and Black struggle. They both fall onto the floor and wrestle. The gun goes off and the struggle ceases. They both stare at each other for a few seconds. Ace checks himself as he stands holding the gun. Black looks down at his body. They both exhale a sigh of relief as they realize neither of them was shot.

I suddenly feel a burning sensation in my stomach so I reach down to soothe it. My shirt feels wet. I look down and see that I'm bleeding. I lose the feeling in my legs and collapse onto the floor. I watch Ace, still holding the gun. He's staring in disbelief as he sees me hold the bleeding wound on my stomach.

"Oh my God! Stormey!" Ace panics as he stands over me before running out of the room. Ace comes back with a towel and uses it to apply pressure to my wound. Black runs out the door.

I lay on the floor in agonizing pain without uttering a word. I can hear him calling for an ambulance, but my thoughts move at lightning speed, causing me to tune out my surroundings. I tried so hard to make my life better, but now I am dying. Nothing in the world makes sense.

Why is joy only fleeting in between moments of pain? Chasing the idea of happiness is what kept me in bondage to my suffering. So, what's the point of any of it? Is this why I was born? To suffer, struggle, and then die?

Each breath becomes harder to take. Then, like lightning, it hits me, *I'm not ready to die.* I remember Aunt Jewel's God and can only hope it's not too late to pray.

God, it's me, Stormey. If you're real, this would be the time to show me because right now it's hard to believe that you are any more than a fairy tale. According to some, you are supposed to be my comforter, but it constantly rains within the walls of my heart and I remain drenched in pain. You have taken so much from me and I can't seem to catch a break. Why did you bring me into this world if all you had for me was misery and suffering? Knowing you in my mind isn't enough. I need you to show up. I don't know who I am or who I am supposed to be. The only thing I know is that I am tired of feeling alone. I don't want to live like this anymore and I don't want to die like this either. I need you. I need you to be REAL. Help me please...

CHAPTER 19

Consciously Unconscious

I am conscious, but not awake. I hear the faint beeping of the heart monitor through the commotion of the doctors as they perform surgery in a collaborative effort to preserve my life. Part of me desperately wants to wake up. The other part doesn't because I've never felt more at peace.

The darkness of the room is dispelled as I hear a faint whisper. "Stormey! Stormey, wake up!"

I slowly rise up from my body and see everything as if it were a movie. I am spirit, looking at my unconscious body lying on the operating table, realizing I am the observer and not the observed.

"Stormey!" I hear the whisper again.

I turn around and see a small girl standing by the door, gesturing with her hands for me to come with her. She looks to be around ten years old. With mahogany skin and curly hair, she has an eerily familiar presence. I follow behind as she opens the door for me to walk through. Once I cross the threshold of the doorway, everything goes pitch black and completely silent. Then out of nowhere, a tumultuous wind blows all around me revealing a deserted town. Everything that's not deeply rooted is vigorously strewn throughout the atmosphere. Terrified, I run to seek shelter, but the wind aggressively pushes and pulls me as I struggle to stay on my feet. I find a building nearby that appears to be sturdy and unaffected by the violent winds.

"Stormey!" The wind whispers. The blood in my body turns cold. Startled, I stumble, falling into the building with my back against the bricks. I close my eyes tightly hoping that when I open them, I will wake up from this horrid nightmare. The wind continues roaring loudly, yet, I can hear the faint sound of a baby's cry. I open my eyes and to my disappointment, I'm still stuck in this place and the wind is even more violent. It's moving faster and stronger, but I can still hear the faint cries of a baby. I look around, trying to locate where the cry is coming from, but it's hard to see because I can barely keep my eyes open with the particles of dirt flying into my face. I see train tracks and what appears to be a buggy or stroller. I try to push myself off the bricks but the wind pushes me back into them. I push off again refusing to be defeated and manage to pull away while fighting for each step I take.

Finally, I reach the buggy, which is sitting in the middle of the train tracks. A small bird sits on the handle chirping as if it's standing guard. It's watching over the infant child wrapped in a purple blanket, wearing a white lace headband. She's crying frantically, hoping to be heard. As I reach in to pick her up and comfort her, the bird flies away as if its job is done.

"How did you get here? Where is your mother? Who left you like this? And why are you on these train tracks?" I ask out loud, not anticipating a response.

I hear the horn of an oncoming train heading right towards us. Startled, I jump off the tracks with the baby, just in time. I watch the train completely demolish the buggy. The infant is still crying hysterically, and I sense her fear. Or maybe she senses mine. We're both afraid.

I hold her closely and rub her back gently as I whisper in her ear comfortingly, "Shh, it's okay. I don't know what happened to you or why you were left here alone, but I'm here now and I've got you. You don't have to worry anymore. I'm not going to let anyone, or anything hurt you." I feel her calming down.

I continue, "You are stronger than you know. We are surviving this storm. Baby, you are special, and you are meant to be here. God has his hands on you, and you are protected. You don't have to be afraid anymore."

I feel the anxiety leave her body as she relaxes. The wind ceases simultaneously with her cries. Soothing her also soothes me. I close my eyes and hug her tightly. The tighter I hug her the more peace I feel within my own body. I open my eyes and see the sun has risen above, clearing the clouds and drying the rain. The dirt has turned into grass. I am alarmed to find the baby is missing from my arms and I am actually wrapping my arms around my own body, holding myself tightly.

I panic and look around frantically to see if I dropped her, but there is no trace of her or the storm. Just ahead I notice the little curly-headed girl that guided me here. She's skipping joyfully through the remaining pastures gesturing for me to join her.

She's swinging her arms, spinning with a smile on her face as if she is free of all burdens. Watching her is calming for me. The wind quiets, the dust turns back into a state of greenery. I take steps towards her and the closer I get the more familiar she becomes. Panic rushes through me as I stand with her face to face. I see clearly now. She is me.

"Keep calm, Stormey," she says. "Haven't you noticed that as your feelings change, the atmosphere does too? When you are in a state of acceptance, beauty, and peace, so is everything around you. When you are in a state of fear, bitterness, and violence, so is the same for everything you see."

I ask, "Are you saying that I'm imagining the weather changing? The storm isn't real?"

"You give it all meaning," she explains.

"Basically, I see everything around me based on what's going on inside of me?"

She nods yes. "Where we are is just a figment of your imagination. This is your soul showing you that you are more powerful than you know. You're going to have to wake up and go back to your life but only you can choose which lens you'll see your life through. Will you continue to be a victim of your circumstances? Will you continue to be angry at others for not choosing you or showing up the way you hoped? Or will you listen to your soul? No matter what has happened to you or is happening around you, you have survived, and you will continue surviving. Stormey, you and me, we are strong. God protected us from all the chaos and therefore, we have nothing to fear," she says. "We are meant to be here."

Clarity hits me like a ton of bricks. This has all been about me. Even the baby I found. That was me finding myself. Everything I said to her, I really said to myself. Seeing the ten-year-old version of myself living so freely and full of joy is a reminder that it's time for me to let go of the baggage of unmet expectations. I need to finally accept the life I was given for what it is and stop wishing for it to be any different. By constantly hoping and wishing for things to be different, I put myself in a position of always seeking that which I do not have and I will never experience happiness that way.

I feel the burdens lift off me as peace seeps into my body because finally I see it's time for me to choose me.

Suddenly, I cannot see. It's pitch black once again.

CHAPTER 20

Back on Purpose

After surviving surgery, I wake up feeling groggy as hell. I can't tell how long my mother's been here or why, for that matter. However, I feel her sitting closely and hear her quietly praying. It's surprising enough, but even more so because she's praying for me. Chills run through me as I listen.

She starts, "Unlike me she has tried her best to stay away from the things that would be displeasing to you, Lord. She is filled with goodness and always strives to be who you said she should be. She is the only thing I've done right in my life and I can't even take credit for that. She's laying here fighting for her life and yet I am the one standing over her praying. This is my Karma. I promise you Lord, if you heal her and bring her through this, I will check myself into rehab today. I will clean myself up and give my life to you. It seems like I could never find any value in myself or any reason to do better, but I see how not living right is a consequence that has ruined everyone that ever loved me. I beg you Father God to please grant me this one request. Please hear me and save her, Lord."

As she notices me moving and attempting to slowly open my eyes to the light, she screams, "Thank you. Thank you. Thank you."

I'm filled with uneasiness, as seeing her express any care or concern for me is unfamiliar. I have no idea what to say or think. Over the years, it's been hard to find love in my heart for her. I could only see reasons to hate her.

I attempt to sit up, but pain shoots through my abdomen, so I slowly press my back into the bed with a grimace and moan.

"Don't try to move, you might pop your stitches," she advises.

I move my hand slowly across my stomach, feeling myself as if for the first time. The bandages and everything under them feels swollen and tender to the touch.

"What are you doing here?" I say, still surprised to see her.

"What do you mean? I came as soon as I heard," she responds.

"How did you know, though?" I ask still confused.

"He told me." She nods her head toward the back of the room.

"I didn't even see him there," I say, surprised to see Jay asleep in the chair across the room.

"Where's Ace?"

"I don't know. Jay will have to tell you that."

"Well, wake him up please," I request.

"Not yet. There are some things I want to talk to you about, if I may."

Trying to divert things from getting too awkward I ask, "When I first woke, did I hear you praying?"

"Yes."

"When did you start, I mean, I didn't know someone like you would believe in God."

"What does that mean...someone like me?"

"Well, Aunt Jewel always said, if you want to know what a person believes, watch their actions. Their words will tell you who they wish to be, but their actions will tell you who they believe they are."

"That sounds like your aunt. She was so wise, but that don't have nothing to do with nothing. If that was the case, then no one would be able to say they believe in God. I believe in God and yet I sin, just like everyone else," she explains.

"It sounded like you were praying for me. Why would you do that?"

"I feel like He is punishing me through the suffering of you and your sister..."

I interrupt her before she finishes. "How did you make this about you? You are so delusional and self-important that you really believe God is orchestrating things just to get you. You know what? Never mind. I'm sorry." I stop myself because I know I'm being mean when she is trying. I remember the message from my dream and I don't want to keep acting out of bitterness.

"Well, it's not that I'm being delusional. How else do you explain me being here in good health after years of self-abuse, yet you all are the ones suffering? I'll tell you how, you all are paying for my sins. I heard God say that if I want to fix my family, I need to fix myself. So, I told Him if he woke you up I'd never get high again and I meant it.

I'm getting clean and I will stay clean this time. This has gone on long enough."

"So just like that, you're going to get clean?"

"Yes, I'm checking myself into a live-in facility on Monday," she says matter-of-factly.

"Well, if it were that easy then why didn't you do it before?"

"To be honest, I felt like everyone was doing better without me. I had no reason to stop."

"And now you do?"

"Yes, now I feel like I have a purpose. That's all I needed, a reason to live better and just simply be better," she continues to explain.

For the first time, she seems sincere. Still surprised, I say, "I hear what you're saying, but I feel like there is more to this. What exactly gave you this new feeling of purpose?"

"There comes a time in a person's life when they know they can't go on like they've been any longer, but knowing isn't enough. They need a reason beyond themselves to make a change. A long time ago I went astray and since then I've failed every test that has been put before me. I've wished to change for so long, but I've never mustered up the strength to do it. I lacked motivation.

"Skye is in jail and you're lying in this bed fighting for your life. This is not the life I imagined for you girls. Jewel was the glue that kept everything together and now that she isn't here, it's all falling apart. You two don't deserve to suffer the sins of your mother. After reading the letter Jewel left for me, it all made sense."

"What letter?" I ask.

"I found a letter inside of Jewel's bible. I'm not sure when she wrote it, but it was written to me."

"What did it say? Did she write me one?" I ask eagerly.

"I only saw the one and it had my name on it."

"Can I see it?" I ask. She reaches into her back pocket, carefully unfolds the pages, and slowly hands it to me as if it's fragile.

My Darling Baby Sister,
I still think about when we were kids and how you used to follow me around and steal my clothes. I used to tell you that you were annoying, but secretly I loved having you look up to me the way you did. I vowed that I would always protect you. However, when I should've stayed, selfishly, I fled. I am sorry that after I left, you too, were molested and abused. I never thought that my leaving would create a

void that needed to be filled. I was only thinking of what was happening to me but didn't consider that I was failing you.

Somehow, I believed that by suffering in silence I was protecting you from suffering too. I now get that I could not do for you what I had not learned to do for myself. Knowing it happened to me first only made it worse because if I had the courage to speak up, I could've stopped it. Instead, I left at the first chance of a better life. For that I am forever sorry.

The guilt of that has haunted me until this day, which is why I will never turn my back on you again. Every single time you call me I show up no matter what. I continuously pray for your healing because I know the pain of life can cut so deeply it feels like you're suffocating. You've endured so much that you tried to numb your pain in ways that only worsened it, which caused a vicious cycle of drug abuse. You've made mistakes and believe we will never forgive you. You think you've fallen too far, that you could never muster the strength to climb your way back. I always knew in my heart that when you were ready, God would answer my prayers and remove the dark cloud over you to let light in. I couldn't be any prouder of you than I am now. You are pulling through for yourself and your girls by getting clean. Leave all of those fearful thoughts behind you because I love you and I forgive you. God loves you and has forgiven you. It's now your turn to forgive yourself. You did the best you could and that's all anyone can expect from you. And now your best is better.

I want to share this message I received while reading Matthew 20:1-16:

God's Grace is equal for everyone. It doesn't matter if you have been diligent in your work all of your life or if you just began. For God wants to share what is His equally with all of his creation. It is His therefore, He does as He wants with it and not what others see fit. So do not worry about the opinions of others regarding what you have done in your life and the choices you have made up until this exact moment. That is none of their business and their opinion about you is none of yours. The only opinion that matters is that of God's and He said the last will be first and the first will be last. It is not too late to step into your greatness. It is not too late to get back on purpose in your life. So, what if you had to stay in the wilderness a little bit longer before finding your way out? In the end the only thing that matters is that YOU FOUND YOUR WAY OUT! Stop listening to folks and believing what they say about you! Tell those that keep bringing up your past that, yes that was me. Yes, I did that! SO WHAT! Today I AM BACK ON PURPOSE!

Amber, you are a strong and courageous woman to take this step, and I want you to know that I will always admire and respect you for being unbreakable. It is now time to release the pains of yesterday and reclaim your life!
I will love you Always,
Your Sister,
Jewel

"I had a low moment and just wanted to feel close to my sister again. I went over to the house and walked into her room. Her Bible was lying on her bed. I reminisced about how she used to touch it when she read every morning and every night. I picked it up and opened it to a random page. This was folded inside as if she knew I was coming and had it there intentionally waiting for me," she explained.

"She has a way of knowing. She was expecting you," I respond.

"I've been clean for eleven days now," she exclaims.

"Really?"

"I haven't had anything, not even a cigarette, since the day she passed," she explains. "Jewel never stopped believing that I would get better. She was the only one that had faith in me. Seeing the only person that I had in my corner die like that in front of me had a sobering effect. Finding this letter shows how deeply she loved and believed in me. She wrote it for the day I decided to get clean, knowing it would come. I can't let her faith go to waste. I owe her that much."

"Wow! I can tell you are serious, I'm actually proud of you."

"Stormey, I know you hate me because I haven't been what I should've been for you, but I truly am sorry and hope one day you'll be able to forgive me. I know this is no excuse, but I felt like I didn't know how to be a mother because I never had one myself."

Here she goes with her excuses. There's always a sob story but I don't understand why she thinks she's the only one with one. Hell, Skye and I have our own because of her and the choices she made that impacted us. Aunt Jewel as well. I want to say this and more, but I feel like Auntie is watching me. I hold my tongue, not wishing to pile on the guilt because that could ruin her chances of getting better.

"Aunt Jewel said we are not the product of our circumstance, we are the product of our decisions," I respond.

"Yes, she is a better woman than I'll ever be," Amber says. "The point I'm making to you is this, people change. Cons become community activists, promiscuous women evolve into wives and mothers. Addicts get clean and counsel others that are where they used to be. Ex-hoodlums are now police officers, attorneys, and judges that mentor troubled youth. Sometimes people go the wrong way and end up right. I want to be one of those people. I want to be better and I'm ready to make the necessary adjustments to become the person Jewel always believed I would be. I hope you will find it in your heart to support me, but if you aren't ready, I understand. I know I royally screwed your lives up and I am sorrier than you will ever know."

I listen to the words flow from her lips and for the first time it feels like her heart is sincere. I used to believe we would someday bury her in an early grave, but now I believe she's ready to change. The emotional heaviness dissipates as compassion creeps into my spirit. This is what forgiveness feels like. I understand what Aunt Jewel meant when she said forgiveness becomes your way you will truly be free. I no longer see Amber as a pathetic junkie. Instead, I see the little girl that never healed.

Overlooking her flaws gives way to overcoming the barrier of judgment wedged between us. Forgiveness was never for her sake, it was for my own peace of mind. And that's what I feel...peace.

I say, "I know I've been hard on you, but that's because you hurt me. I understand you were hurt by the people you loved and trusted, but that doesn't justify you hurting the ones that loved and trusted you. I longed for you, but whenever I allowed myself to get close, your bitterness would ooze out of you and pour onto me.

"You made me feel like I wasn't good enough because you chose drugs over me. I had to disconnect myself from you and it's hard for me to even think about allowing you back into my life or my heart because I already mourned the idea of you, even though you were alive. I see that you're ready to reinvent yourself and I do want to be around to see you pull it off. I want to get to know the new you. So, I guess what I'm saying is, I think this is my first time really seeing you and I forgive you."

"Stormey, I had a troubled heart and mind long before I was pregnant with you or your sister. I didn't plan on having you and I was not prepared to be a mother. I wanted to care, I was just too screwed up to do right. Even though having children was a blessing, it could never cure my addiction. That required a strength I just didn't have.

Hearing those words from you means more to me than you know. I promise I am going to get better and make new memories with you that will replace the bad ones," she replies excitedly while wrapping her arms around me.

I hug her back softly, trying not to raise my arms too high. It feels so strange to embrace her like this. We haven't done this since I was a child. I release my arms from around her as she is holding me longer than I can tolerate. She is visibly overwhelmed with emotions and cries.

Jay wakes up from his sleep and asks, "What's going on? Everything okay?"

"Yeah, everything's actually better than okay," Amber responds.

"I'm happy to see you're awake. You scared me." Jay kisses my hand.

"I guess this just means it's not my time yet," I say.

"Well, I'm glad because I still have plans for you," he says smiling.

"Thank you for being here. It means a lot."

"You know I have your back. I couldn't leave your side until I knew you were straight."

"Has Ace been here?" I ask.

"Nah, that nigga's lucky he's in custody."

"What do you mean he's in custody? For what?"

"What do you mean for what? He's the reason you're in here," he states angrily.

"No, he isn't. Black is the one that shot me. Do the police think it was Ace?" I panic.

"Black shot you?" Jay stutters over his thoughts.

"Black pointed his gun at me, Ace grabbed it, they fought, and I got shot. Black ran and Ace stayed with me," I explain.

"Well, it may be best they have Ace locked up right now, if that's the case. If I know Black, he isn't done with him."

"Oh my God! This is like a a nightmare. I need to talk to the police and tell them what really happened. I need you to call and let them know I'm awake and I need to talk."

"I'm sure the nurses will let them know you are awake. I think they have some sort of obligation. I'm sorry, Stormey." Jay holds my hand tightly. "Don't worry, Black will pay for what he did to you. I guarantee it."

"Jay, don't go being a vigilante on account of me. You're only going to make things worse. You will end up killing him, going to jail, or getting yourself killed. There is no winning scenario going about it like that. Let the police handle Black."

"Stormey, you are too important for me to let this ride," Jay expresses.

"For someone who's always talking about getting married, how do you expect to do that from a grave or jail cell?"

"There you go making sense again. You always get me together, don't you? That's how I know you're Wifey," he reiterates and rubs my hair.

"You know what, Jay? I couldn't imagine life without you. You really are good to me."

Jay replies, "Is that your way of telling me you love me, Stormey?"

"That's my way of saying you've always had my back. You've never held it over my head nor asked for anything in return. Of course I love you."

"I love you more," Jay responds, looking handsome with a heart-warming smile and a twinkle in his eyes.

"Before you go to sleep, look at this," Amber says as she hands me her cell phone. "It's an in-patient rehab facility that's affiliated with this hospital. I'm going to see if I can enroll."

Before I close my eyes, I look around the room. Everything seems brighter. I feel lighter while smiling from the inside out. I recognize this moment as the onset of joy.

CHAPTER 21

Here Comes Reign

"Stormey, Stormey, Stormey. Can't you see, something 'bout your eyes just hypnotize me. And I just love your righteous ways, guess that's why I hope, you'll see some day." Jay enters the room singing to the rhythm of *Hypnotize* by Notorious B.I.G.

"Dude, you're the funniest," I chuckle, "I thought you left."

"When I heard you were being discharged today, I went to the store to get you something to wear." He hands me a bag.

I look inside and there's a yellow Adidas jogging suit with a pair of sneakers to match. "You remembered. I love yellow. You didn't have to do this."

"I know, but I couldn't let you leave out of here wearing that gown because the clothes you came in here with are busted."

"Yeah, you're right. Thank you." I go into the bathroom to change out of the hospital gown. While walking past the mirror I catch a glimpse of myself and I barely recognize my own reflection. I look tired, older, and worn out. I've spent so many days feeling sorry for myself because I felt like no one had stuck around or showed up.

My mother, father, Skye, and even Aunt Jewel all abandoned me in one way or another. I wanted so badly for someone to say, *Stormey, you matter, and I choose you.* Having never received the love and acceptance I desperately desired, I continued searching for all that I thought was missing.

Aunt Jewel tried to get me to understand that my perspective of the world was more important than anything that was happening. She always said I couldn't win in life if I was losing in my mind. I naively blew her off thinking I had it all figured out. I spent most of my days believing that the circumstances of my life were constantly breaking me down, but it wasn't. The reality is, everything I experienced broke me open and it can build me up if I let it.

No one can save me from the battle I've been fighting within myself. Had it not been for my mother and Skye leaving me all alone, then Aunt Jewel would've never taken me with her. Who knows what I would've been doing just to survive.

As I reflect, I'm interrupted by my cell phone ringing. I don't recognize the number on the caller ID.

"Hello?" I answer, hoping it's Ace.

"Hello, my name is Amanda and I'm calling from The Art Museum. Is this Stormey?"

"Yes, this is she," I answer.

"Great! I'm calling regarding The Aspiring Young Artist Competition. We received your submission and I'm pleased to say you're one of the finalists," the woman says.

"Wait, I didn't apply to..." I start to say.

"Congratulations! You now have the chance to win a cash scholarship to The Art University. Ms. Jewel Knights filled out the form," she continues.

So, that's what she did with the painting I gave her. "Oh my God! Is this real? Is this really happening right now?"

"What?" Jay whispers.

I cover the phone with my hand and whisper, "I may get a scholarship to an art school!"

She continues, "Yes, Stormey! It really is. On the twenty-first we're hosting a dinner for our donors at the Art Museum at six in the evening. We hope you will join us as we reveal our scholarship winners."

"Of course I'll be there!"

"Awesome! When we hang up, I'll send you an email with the details. We look forward to seeing you."

"Thank you."

"You're very welcome and good luck to you," she says before hanging up.

"Oh my God!" I scream.

"That's dope!" Jays responds.

"I can't believe Aunt Jewel submitted my painting and didn't tell me. Even in passing she's still a blessing to me. I feel like this is a sign. I have a strong sense that I might actually win this."

"Stormey, you're the most talented person I know. You definitely got it." He hugs me and says, "I'm proud of you. I'll carry your stuff down and get the car."

"Okay, I'll come down to the front," I reply. "Before I go home can you take me to the police precinct to pick up Skye and Ace? I feel bad that Ace had to stay in jail until I came out of surgery and was coherent enough to make a statement."

"Yeah, I couldn't imagine being in there for something I didn't do," Jay says as he walks out.

As we arrive at the precinct I say, "Thank you, Jay, for the ride. Will you wait for us?"

"Of course. You don't have to thank me. You know I got you," Jay replies.

"You're a really good friend," I say as I lean in and give him a hug.

"Yeah, I am," he replies with a smile.

I walk into the police station where a young female officer is sitting. "Good afternoon. I'm here for Skye Knights and Ace King. They both are in your jail."

"I need your ID and for you to fill out this bond paperwork. What's your name?" Officer Reign asks.

"My name is Stormey Knights," I answer. "You look so young to be an officer. How old are you?"

"I'm twenty-four," she says while looking over my paperwork.

"You're just a little older than me. I didn't realize you could be an officer so young. I'm used to seeing old men."

"You can be one as young as twenty-one actually," she states.

"What made you want to become one?"

She chuckles, "The best way to effect change is to be in a position of power. This is my way of making my mark on the world and doing my best to hold the people around me accountable."

"Wow, that's awesome. You go, Girl! You're so inspiring. I hope to make my mark on the world as well," I say.

"Have a seat while I get them for you," Officer Reign instructs.

"Getting up and down causes me quite a bit of pain so I'll stand if it's not going to be too long," I say.

"No problem. I'll be right back," she steps away.

After waiting an hour, the door opens and I see Ace looking disheveled. I walk up to him and wrap the one arm I can lift around him. "I was so worried about you." I try not to cry.

"You were worried about me? I was worried about you," he says. "How are you?"

"Better now. Do you know what happened to Black?" I ask.

"He's on the run but it's only a matter of time before he gets what's coming to him," Ace replies.

A few moments later Skye walks out looking like she hasn't bathed or combed her hair in days. "Girl, I'm so glad to be out of there!" Skye exclaims.

"I'm so happy you are, too. I can't believe that buzzard did this to you!"

"It's all good, he's going to get what he deserves," Skye responds.

"Well don't say too much, we are still in the police station," I warn.

"Yeah, you're right. Let's get out of here," Ace states.

"If you need money for a lawyer or anything, the money Auntie left us should help."

"Aunt Jewel always did take care of us," Skye smiles softly.

"Well, you know she left both of us the house too so you can get your stuff from Troy's and move in ASAP."

"I was thinking the same thing," Skye concurs.

As we exit the building, I hesitate as the sun immediately brushes my skin with its velvety warmth. It feels so good. I take it all in. Everything feels different. After carrying emotional baggage for so long it feels good to finally feel free.

I now know that we carry with us two kinds of emotional pain. There's purposeful pain that causes growth and results in us becoming stronger. Then there's futile pain which keeps us stuck and results in our suffering. I wallowed around in the latter like a pig in mud for years, wearing it proudly like a badge of honor. The filth of it showed up in everything. I couldn't see anything or anyone clearly because my perspective was tainted.

Nothing could make me happy and nothing was ever good enough because I never believed I was enough. I have no more tolerance for emotional bondage. Finally, I can release the familiar pain stemming from the perception of brokenness, heartbreak, and loneliness.

I have no more space for the agony of unmet expectations of those who I thought failed me. I forgive everyone who's hurt me. I forgive myself for believing they possessed the power to do so. I forgive each person who abandoned me when I needed them. I forgive myself for believing I needed someone else to save me. I release it all as I regain control of my life.

As the wind sweeps through the trees, I think of my dream and I hear Aunt Jewel's words echo in my mind: "Your thoughts are prayers. Whatever you focus on tends to show up in your life. Focus on the life and peace that you want and ignore what you don't."

I don't know the ending to my story, but I'm no longer scared. I'm joyous in committing to my vision with an open mind and open heart. From this day forward I commit to myself to always remember that I'm not the things I've done. I'm not the things that were done to me. I'm not the neighborhood nor circumstances I grew up in. I'm not my parents, nor their mistakes. I'm more than a fatherless daughter born to a drug-addicted mother. I'm more than a girl with a broken heart, a pain in my chest, or worry in my stomach. I'm more than all I've claimed to be.

I am what I believe. I am how I lead. I am how I love. I am how I serve. And I am worthy of everything I dream.

My name is Stormey Knights and I'm rewriting my story.

About Vibes: We are an independent publishing company that believes writers should only have to worry about writing. Meaning, you write your book, we'll do the rest.

To learn more about us, our authors, and their books, please visit us at

Writeandvibe.com | Fb & IG @writeandvibe

ABOUT THE AUTHOR

Dominique Krystal Dawn is a sage that uses creative storytelling to dive deeper into the personal motivations and pain point perspectives masked as ordinary life decisions. She was born and raised in Cleveland, Ohio, where she learned the tough spiritual lessons that each soul must grow through. Dominique desires to reignite hope and facilitate healing and self-realization in each reader so that despite their beginning, they can get back on purpose and live a fulfilling life.

CPSIA information can be obtained
at www.ICGtesting.com
Printed in the USA
LVHW010458180723
752701LV00003B/423